D0291940

✓

SEP 90

PAPER
PRODUCTS

PAPER PRODUCTS

STORIES BY

James W. Hall

W·W·NORTON & COMPANY
NEW YORK · LONDON

The text of this book is composed in Garamond,
with display type set in Copperplate Gothic.
Composition and manufacturing by The Haddon Craftsmen, Inc.
Book design by Jo Anne Metsch.

First Edition

Library of Congress Cataloging-in-Publication Data
Hall, Jim, 1947–
Paper products : stories / by James W. Hall.—1st ed.
p. cm.
I. Title.
PS3558.A369P37 1990
813'.54—dc20

ISBN 0-393-02824-0

W. W. Norton & Company, Inc., 500 Fifth Avenue, New York, N. Y. 10110
W. W. Norton & Company Ltd., 37 Great Russell Street, London WC1B 3NU
1 2 3 4 5 6 7 8 9 0

CONTENTS

ACKNOWLEDGMENTS

The author gratefully acknowledges the following magazines in which these stories first appeared:

> *Carolina Quarterly*: "The Miracles"
> *Georgia Review*: "Paper Products," "Gas"
> *Iowa Review*: "Miami Beach, Kentucky"
> *Kenyon Review*, "Survival Week"
> *Missouri Review*: "Poetic Devices"
> *Panache*: "An American Beauty"
> *Wisconsin Review*: "The Electric Poet"

Further appreciation is due the Fine Arts Council of Florida for financial assistance which provided time to complete these stories.

PAPER
PRODUCTS

GAS

She'd thought it would be a gas to come home to Buck's Gap and put up a show. Visit her dad, shock the natives, maybe walk through a field, pick wild flowers, goofy rural stuff. Then get back to L.A. and tell Buck's Gap stories for the next six months. But here she was in her dad's kitchen baking dog biscuits.

Warhol, the family's ancient retriever, had lost his teeth. Now kibbles were too hard, wet food had some kind of ash or something that stirred up his liver problems, and the special vet food was too expensive. So she'd modified her chocolate chip cookie recipe, dumping crumbs of ground round into the batter and then forming the nuggets into bone shapes. And now Warhol was addicted to them, nosing her in the butt from the minute she got up around noon till four the next morning, prompting her to hand over another baked bone.

Her Clothing-Art Show was supposed to go on at five-thirty that afternoon at Farmers Bank and Trust, and here she was at five o'clock peeking in the oven, trying to keep Warhol blissed out.

Her dad had been just as bad. The whole three days she'd been home, he'd been tagging along behind her soon as she was up, planting himself in the same room with her, carrying along whatever he was whittling at the moment. Droning on in that hillbilly voice about whatever batted through his mind. She loved him, sure, but sometimes he was too country to take seriously. Somewhere between Gomer Pyle and Li'l Abner.

She'd not walked through a single field since she'd come home, so busy baking bones and cleaning up her dad's little piles of shavings. At that moment he was sanding the edges and grooves of a chunk of walnut the size of a baseball, shaped into a perfect replica of a human brain.

"Kuru," he said, while Warhol swept his tail across the kitchen floor, flat on his stomach, looking up at her. "Kuru's a disease the affects only the natives of New Guinea."

"Daddy-O," she said, turning the temperature off on the oven, "I got to get my things together for the show."

"It's a disease of laughter. They begin laughing and can't stop, can't eat, can't sleep or drink water or make love. I'd heard of hiccuping to death, but this I hadn't heard of till I saw it on the TV. Damnedest thing."

"It's wild all right," Tina Blue said. "Now I got to get my act in gear. You're coming, right?"

Her father pulled his penknife out of his pants pocket, opened it, dug out a small trail along the top of the brain.

"I hadn't got this medulla oblongata just right." He shook his head, frowned at the brain. "Course I'm coming, Tina Blue. Course."

"You'll freak," she said.

"I bet I will."

Tina Blue spent from five to five-fifteen stacking and spraying her black hair and studded the whole goopy mess with feathers and rhinestones. She put on a leopard leotard, then an aquamarine and fuchsia nun's robe on top. She carried a small leather shield that was actually a purse. She called it "the bicoastal-gladiator-bag." She'd put on a few rubber rings and a necklace she'd made from the shells of dime-store turtles.

"That's a getup," her father said as she came into the living room. She did a modeling spin, then a robot mechanical walk. The L.A. high tech strut.

On their way down to the bank, her dad driving the Hudson he'd kept alive all these years, Tina Blue picked up her father's walnut brain from the seat and turned it this way and that.

"Dad, you're weirder than I am."

"Naw," he said.

"Why'd you want to do a brain?"

"I'm interested in them," he said. "That disease, kuru?"

"Yeah?"

"I wouldn't mind going that way, you know." He stopped in the middle of the street. No traffic light, no stop sign. Tina Blue turned to check out the back window. A car had stopped behind them. The man waited a minute, then passed them slowly, smiling at her daddy and saying howdy.

"But the only way the New Guineas get kuru is by eating human brains."

"Jesus, Daddy-O."

"I draw the line there. Not even to die laughing."

He put the Hudson Wasp in gear and started off again.

"It's funny," she said. "In New York the audiences were frigid. I called them SoHo cool. They walk in, not saying a word about the show, drink champagne, all of them dressed to the tenth power, very intellectually distant. Nobody wanting to crack a pose. It's like a high school party when everybody was afraid to blow it. Out in L.A., man, they say whatever they think. Great things like 'These are the kind of things a mass murderer has nightmares about.' Or like how the only people who could actually wear clothes like mine would be the guys fighting for the Martian heavyweight wrestling championship. They get in there and try to outdo each other with smart remarks. I love it."

"I guess why I do it," he said, "carving so many brains, when you get right down to it, it's because of how Freddy Red turned out."

"Oh, God," Tina Blue groaned.

Freddy Red was her older brother. He'd been born with cretinism, some kind of thyroid disorder. Wide, flat saddle nose, tongue always hanging out, bloated belly, skin as coarse as a cedar plank, and thick hands and fingers. He was off in West Virginia, living in a big hospital for people like him. Tina Blue had never visited him 'cause, she told herself, she didn't want to stir him all up. She'd maybe said three words to him when she was little, just learning to talk, before they sent him off.

Her father said, "It's given me an interest in brains."

She set the brain on the seat between them and looked out her window at the dogwoods blooming, the jonquils, the bright new shoots. In L.A. she'd forgotten about spring. Maybe, in a way, living in a place without a spring had given her creations more flare, sprouting all those impossible colors and textures and wild, capricious shapes and mixtures of traditions. Yeah, maybe she'd say something like that today at the bank, jazz up these hayseeds' vision of themselves. Because the corollary was that if you lived in a place like Buck's Gap that had a fantastic spring, then you let your own brain get drab, you put yourself in neutral, let nature do all your imagining for you. No, that might be too much of an overload for the audience of Buck's Gappers.

"I wished we hadn't moved around so much," her father said. He'd stopped again in the middle of Main Street, right in front of the Kiddie Korner Klothing Store, and the little traffic that there was, Buck's Gap rush hour, was flowing peacefully around them.

"I'm going to be late, Daddy-O," Tina Blue said.

"It was the only way I knew of making money. Fixing up a dump and selling it for double what I paid for it. It was a good income, but it wasn't any way to raise a family. I always thought it was why your mama run off. Never settled. Soon as we'd get the floorboards patched so you could walk through the house without falling through, we'd be out on the front porch, handing over the key to somebody."

"It was OK, Daddy-O. I liked it fine."

"I think how some people live their whole life in the same house. Maybe even the same house where their daddy or mama was born. And I think of us, how we never let the dust settle but we were on to the next one."

"You been living in that one house now for five years. That's a long while," Tina Blue said.

"It's rented. That's somebody else's floor, their roof, their toilet. I'm renting their mirrors and sinks. I might as well be living at the bus depot."

Tina Blue raised the alligator-skin lid of her watch. Quarter till six. Fifteen minutes after the show was supposed to begin. The clothes were hung already, back near the main vault, but still, she should be there. At least to hear the corn pone brains react.

"I'm glad we lived how we lived, Daddy-O. It gave me angst, a sense of outsiderness. Everybody feels that way in cities; it's existential. Not feeling at home in the universe. I got a head start on it, and it's why I'm an artist. If we'd just lived in one house and had a safe, predictable, static life, I'd still be here in Buck's Gap probably, somebody's wife, living in the same house for the rest of my life. Going to see an art-to-wear show by some weird girl from L.A. Having no imagination myself, no unease. Nothing to overcome. You see what I'm saying, Daddy-O?"

He put the car in gear again, got under way, and said, "I wish I'd never sent Freddy Red off. I wished I had him near me now. I just got that old dog, not worth a damn."

"You got me, Daddy-O, what do you mean, you don't have anybody?"

Her daddy smiled, and she thought for a minute he was going to stop again in the street, so she didn't give him a smile back. He slowed, looking over at her, but kept on going.

At the bank there was a crowd.

Tina Blue flowed in through the double glass doors. An old security guard bowed to her, seemed to consider clapping for a moment, then lowered his hands. The crowd opened for her, their murmuring dying out.

"Bravo!" someone called out.

"Speech!" a woman's voice chimed in.

The bank president was waiting for her back in the center

of the exhibit. He stood next to an aluminum bathrobe that had Japanese Christmas lights for a belt. Next to where it was fixed to the wall was her winter collection of men's undershorts made from long red shag carpets with plastic fruit buried away inside the shag.

Her creations were strung up on the wall where usually a collection of old black-and-white photos were hung. They were the earliest photographs ever taken of Main Street and this or that wooden building or muddy street in Buck's Gap. Daddy-O's daddy had taken them back when photography was right up there with dynamiting at the quarry for dangerous jobs.

The president of the bank introduced her to Milton Mosley, the vice-president. Tina Blue shook his hand, and Milton reminded her that he'd sat behind in geometry almost twenty years back. She shook her head at him and smiled wanly. If her L.A. friends had heard that, wow, a guy from geometry class, how sweet.

The president cleared his throat and raised his arms to quiet the crowd.

"Would you like to say a few words, Tina Blue? I'm sure we'd all be edified by anything you might want to say to us."

"Do you see your work as a paradigm for the way contemporary technological models have subverted the simplicity and practical beauty of American life?" someone called out from the group.

A man in overalls had worked to the front of the gathering. He handed her a program the bank had printed up, showing photos of her work, and the man asked her to sign it. "My daughter's got her sewing machine going a hundred miles an hour since she seen this brochure. Me and her mama are right happy about the things she's putting out. Nothing as good as this, but she's sure full of spit and fury."

As Tina Blue autographed the farmer's program, Milton Mosley said, "There's a danger"—watching her carefully—"in creating something that hovers between the caprice and nobility of art and the utilitarian, don't you think?"

"Oh, I totally disagree," the president of the bank said. "Your terms of discussion are outmoded. Luck and accident are the main engines of the new quantum universe. Usefulness is no more than a stage in the life of any material. Leave your after-shave bottle open on the shelf overnight and you'll see how quickly what was once of use can still exist but have no use."

"I think what he means," said an old woman in a berry-covered hat, "is that a shovel that pretends to be a shovel but is only a counterfeit can be dangerous to those who are depending on its being a real shovel."

"It would seem to me," said Milton Mosley, "that art which announces itself as preposterous, which sniggers, has destroyed the tacit agreement between creator and audience. We don't need to be slapped awake by shag carpet underwear; we need to be entranced by some new entertainment which is only a cockeyed and illuminating degree or two off what the past has prepared us for. Art which mocks and swaggers is not art at all, but public farting, don't you think?"

The bank president straightened his striped tie and said, "Look here, if we are to be true to a world in which radical mutants reach out to take some new frightening pathways into the evolutionary future, we must . . ."

Tina Blue backed away from the argument, watched the crowd heal up around her absence. She found her father

talking to the security guard near the front doors.
He had brought his walnut brain inside and was showing
it to the guard.

"Your father is a very weird man," the security guard
said to her when she was beside them.

A feather had worked loose from her sticky hair and was
dangling down across her forehead. She could feel the
sweat running between her breasts. The leotards were
mashing her uncomfortably.

She held her breath for a moment and listened to new
voices speaking from the crowd. The argument had shifted,
and fresh opinions were being expressed. Tina Blue smiled
uncertainly at her father.

"I'd like to go home," she said.

Her father said, "I never seen this bunch so worked up
before. Have you, Billy?"

"Not since that Cherokee Indian with those dogs that
could quote poetry."

"Oh, yeah. That. That was hokum," her father said. "I
was disappointed to see everybody fall for that fellow."

"I heard them dogs," Billy said to Tina Blue. " 'Where
ignorant armies clash by night.' I heard it coming from that
spaniel's own throat."

"I liked to died laughing, myself," said her daddy.

Billy said to Tina Blue, "But it wasn't nothing to compare
to your handiwork. Not by a long way. My goodness, this'll
be the talk of Buck's Gap for years to come."

Milton Mosley came to call on her at seven the next
night. He'd telephoned the evening after her show to apol-
ogize for his attack on her artwork. Her work had had such
an effect on him, he said, such an intoxicating effect that he

wasn't entirely responsible for the outburst. It was OK, Tina Blue said. She didn't take it personally. She was glad for any kind of reaction. But you seemed dizzy and upset when you left, Milton Mosley had said. And Tina Blue replied that yes, she'd been a bit dizzy, but it was from the change in altitude, nothing more.

So he came for her in his long black Ford phaeton.

Tina Blue stood at a front window handing out bones to Warhol, staring at this man getting out of that otherworldly car. He wore a black shirt that had a single red slice of watermelon printed on a pocket, and a pair of black pants and red tennis shoes.

"What is this?" she said.

And her father sitting at the dining-room table, concentrating on his medulla oblongata, said, "He wearing that watermelon shirt?"

"Yes," Tina said.

"Oh, boy. Look out tonight."

"What?"

"Means he's going to ask you to marry him. Wears that every time. Asked every woman south of the Ohio River and always wears that shirt."

Tina gave Warhol the last bone and slipped out the front door before he could begin begging for more.

"Hi," Milton said, standing on the sidewalk, looking too young and too nimble-eyed to be the vice-president of a bank.

"You planning on asking me to marry you, you better just do it now."

"OK," he said. "I never met anyone like you. Ever. I don't think there is anyone like you, Tina Blue. I've asked many a woman to marry me, but I never asked anyone the likes of you. And I can't ever remember when I hoped a woman said yes more than right now. I'm probably not what you had in mind for a husband, but there isn't a thing I wouldn't do to make you happy.

"And the fact is, I make a lot of money, I got a lot put away, and I wouldn't mind letting you spend every penny of it if that was what you wanted. I kiss good. I been told I can make a chunk of marble groan, the way I do some things. And the woman I marry is the last woman I'd ever want."

After the wedding they spent two weeks in California, cleaning out her apartment and seeing all her friends. Milton charmed them all. He softened his hick accent just enough and asked lots of questions and nodded and made a lot of eye contact and stuck in a one-liner here and there, and her girl friends would come up afterward and say, "And he's rich, too?"

They drove up to the wine country and then to Sausalito, and he hadn't lied about making marble groan. Tina Blue and he returned to Buck's Gap in July, and she was warm and sleepy in a way she'd never been.

They bought a big house out on Buck's Lake, five white columns across the front, a big terrace, sugar maples, and Chinese elms. And her daddy moved into the servant's quarters out back.

"I want Freddy Red near me," he said to her one morning in August while she was changing a bobbin on her Singer. She'd been designing a cocktail dress made from the covers of *New Yorker* magazines that she'd enclosed in plastic pouches. But it hadn't been going right. It seemed ludicrous to her. Absurd in a way that a three-headed baby might be absurd. Pointless and grotesque.

"I want him here in this big house where he'll be happy.
Where we can be a happy family for once. I'm not happy. I
never been happy. Never, ever. I sent my son off to live
with idiots and morons, and I regretted it every day of my
life."

Tina Blue stared at her father, glanced back at the cover
of one of those magazines. A dog walking through a snowstorm. She had no idea what *that* meant. Why was *that* a
cover?

"You're happy, Milton's happy. Most every damn person
in this town is happy, at least part of the time. But I'm not.
Because my son's locked away."

"I'll ask Milton," Tina Blue said, still looking at that stupid dog walking through that snowstorm. The dog was a
watercolor blue. Blue? What in the world was that about?

Freddy Red moved into the downstairs bedroom and
took up a position in front of the little black-and-white TV
that Tina's father had bought. He listened to the news channel all day. He told Tina that he was following the desperate
situation in the Middle East and it was very important to
him not to be interrupted. "They need Eisenhower on this
one," he said. "I'm doing the best I can, but a general is
what's needed here." He waited for her reply, watching her
with his blurry gray eyes, and when she said nothing, he
went away into the screen.

Her father seemed happy now. He was at work whittling
a small intestine, a tangle of cedar, loops, and whorls and
corrugated surfaces. He sat out on the back porch within
listening range of Freddy Red's TV and sliced and
smoothed those guts and chuckled to himself as if he had
been nibbling on human brains.

A few days after Freddy Red's arrival, Milton came into Tina Blue's workroom before he left for work. She was sitting at her Singer, feeding a hemline through the slot. She was almost finished with the *New Yorker* dress.

"I'm going to be late tonight," he told her. "There's a show at the bank this afternoon."

Tina Blue watched the gold thread stitching into the shiny orange fabric. She asked him what it was.

"Some gentleman from New York City who collects the bloody clothes from famous assassinations. He has Kennedy's shirt and two presidential candidates' undershirts. A lot of other things with blood on it, too, but I didn't pay that much attention."

"Why didn't you invite me to come?" Tina Blue said. She halted the sewing machine and swiveled to see how Milton would answer this.

"Bloodstains? You want to see a clothesline full of bloodstains?"

"Maybe."

"Well, come then. I just didn't think you'd care about such things."

When he'd gone, she sat still, deeply, densely depressed. She pulled the dress up and found that cover of the dog in the snowstorm. Blue dog, white storm. Icy blue, pure white. It made her sadder still, seeing that dog so hopeless, wandering like that without any idea of which way was home.

It was lost, but still noble somehow. How had anyone been able to draw that? How had anybody known how to pour all those feelings into that one dog, that very ordinary snowstorm? Now that was art. That was the deep song of the soul.

Warhol shuffled into the room, looking for her. He put his head in her lap and made it heavy. This moment, with the TV babbling, the soft slur of her father's knife, his quiet laughter, Warhol's heavy head. This moment hurt her deep and true. But she had not cultivated the skill to hold and love this sorrow. She had learned to zing, but she could not sing.

For several moments her tears dripped onto the dog's nose. She drew the dress from the machine, undressed, and put it on. It was heavy and hot, and when she moved, it made a noise like snow tires on summer pavement. But she kept it on, walking into Freddy Red's room and sitting in the lounge chair beside his. He glanced over at her, studied one or two of the covers, raised his eyebrows, and turned back to the TV.

"Freddy Red," she said, "there's a show at the bank today."

"Yeah?" He watched a press-on fingernail commercial, narrowing his eyes when the demonstration began.

"It's just a bunch of bloody clothes," she said. "But it might be good to get out. Show off my new dress."

"You going to wear that?" he said without looking away from the TV.

"I thought I would," she said. "I never wore anything I made before."

"I ain't going nowhere with you looking like some kind of crazy lady."

"Freddy Red!"

"You hadn't said beans to me for all my life; then you want to take me out and show me off while you wear a dress like that. No way. No way in hell."

"If I wear blue jeans?"

"What else?"

"A work shirt?"

"What else?"

The news anchor came on, backed by a map of the Middle East. Then film began playing of tanks rolling across the desert. And he was gone again, gabbling quietly about Eisenhower.

When Tina returned to her sewing room, she found Warhol dead on the rag rug. His mouth and eyes were open. There was a drool of bloody foam that ran a foot from his mouth. She knelt beside him and ran her hand across his lumpy head, watching for for any rise in his chest.

In a while she had him wrapped in that ridiculous dress in her arms, and she carried him out onto the porch, where her father was chuckling at a particularly humorous twist in his cedar intestines. Tina Blue walked down to the edge of the lake and laid Warhol in the tall grass. She returned to the house for a shovel.

It took her over an hour to dig what she considered a decent hole. By that time her father had noticed her and had joined her. He helped her lower the dog into the hole and squatted down beside her as she tucked the edges of that dress around the carcass.

"I guess that's the end of that," he said. And something between a sputter and a harsh laugh broke from him.

Tina Blue put her arm around his shoulder. Her eyes weren't working right. Some kind of static was blurring them. A hot bubble was growing in her throat.

She stood and hefted the shovel, running her hands up and down the smooth oak handle, feeling the narrowing and thickening of the wood. She found a good grip on it and took a full spadeful of dark earth, lifted it, and let it fall into the hole.

MIAMI BEACH, KENTUCKY

"*I* love it," he said. "I think it's a superb idea." He poured the last of the Schlitz into the peanut jar glass with the clowns on it. Normally that was my glass, but every time Thornton Blanding came to eat dinner with us, he claimed it and made a great show of drinking his beer from it.

"You see," Mean Buck said to Billie Butterworth. "It's not some crackbrained idea. Thornton likes it."

"I never said I like it, Buck. I said I love it. I think it's just what Sinking Fork needs at this particular juncture."

Billie Butterworth fiddled with a carrot stick. She drew a circle with it through the gravy left on her plate.

"May I be excused?" said Lily.

Thornton Blanding rose as Lily stood up. He smiled and

nodded at her like they'd just had a long waltz together. Lily was my sister, two years older than I was, white blond hair that she'd let get long recently, and green eyes that at that moment she'd turned to red to show Thornton Blanding that no amount of standing up or gentlemanly nonsense was going to win her over. She could make those eyes into any color she chose, and it was her gift to be able to burn people with them, brand them good, and walk away leaving them wondering what the hell happened.

Billie Butterworth, my mother, stood then and began to gather up the supper plates. I stayed put, though normally it was my job to scrape the plates. All the rules changed when Thornton Blanding came to supper.

"You don't want any blueberry cobbler, girl?" Mean Buck asked Lily. "Your mama made it up special."

Lily turned her eyes on him and gave him a taste of them. They were drifting back to green, only a dash of scarlet left.

"I lost my appetite."

Mean Buck got up and opened up two more Schlitzes and topped up that clown glass. He and Thornton sat and smiled at each other, though it seemed to me that Mean Buck's smile flowered up from a place a little deeper down than Thornton's.

"You only want to encourage Buck so you can write about the folly of it later. We know just how you work, Thornton. Think of us as naive country folk if you will, but we can see straight on through you."

"Miss Butterworth, it's not so. That's highly unfair. I do admit that Buck's schemes have often provided me with some excellent material, but I truly believe that renaming Sinking Fork to Miami Beach is a remarkable, imaginative, and bold idea."

29

"Miami Beach, Kentucky," pronounced Mean Buck. Beer foam fluttered on his red upper lip.

"Bold," said Billie Butterworth from the stove, where the cobbler was warming and sending out waves of buttery flavor. "It's loony, degrading, and pathetic."

"Why, Miss Butterworth, I can remember vividly you telling us years ago in your art class that we had to cut the mooring lines of our imaginations and float out to the deep, dangerous waters. Those, I believe, were your very words. Out into the deep, dangerous waters."

"I was wrong," she said, and opened up the oven.

"I'm going full blast on this thing starting tomorrow," said Mean Buck.

"Who wants ice cream?"

Everybody did.

Thornton Blanding and Mean Buck went into the library after dessert to drink brandy and chortle. Lily came back into the kitchen and had some cobbler while Billie and I washed the dishes.

"Why do you let him come to supper all the time?" Lily asked.

"He's lonely."

"He gets Mean Buck stirred all up."

"Your daddy was stirred up long before Thornton came back home. And anyway, I'd rather have them here where I can hear what mischief Thornton is putting him up to."

"I read one of his books," Lily announced.

Billie put down her dishrag and went over to the kitchen table, where Lily was scooping up the last flake of cobbler crust. She sat down next to Lily and let go of a sigh that could have filled a balloon.

"Which one did you read?"

"The last one."

"Where'd you get ahold of it?"

"I ordered it at the card shop."

"You ordered it."

"I wanted to find out about him," she said. "I read it, and now I can't see how you can let that man into the house. He hates all of us. He pokes fun at Mean Buck so bad I don't see how he hasn't shot Thornton dead a hundred times."

"Your daddy doesn't read his books, says why should he, he already lived out the stories in them."

I kept on scrubbing at my clown glass, trying to get his lips off it, the beer smell.

"He ought to be sat down and made to read one of them."

"Thornton is using the only subject he has. He's writing the best books he knows how to."

"You haven't read his books if you can defend him like that."

"I've read everything the boy has written."

"People read about us and think we're a bunch of morons from the moron museum. He lies about us, Mama."

"He exaggerates."

"Why'd he come back here anyway? If he likes Hollywood so much, he should've stayed out there."

"He came back here 'cause these are his roots."

"So he could mock us more," said Lily.

"Sinking Fork is his home. He can live here if he wants."

"He got out of here and he should've stayed out. When I leave, I sure ain't ever coming back here. I know better than that."

Thornton and Mean Buck came out of the study guffawing like they were choking on chicken bones. Lily got up

31

quickly, rinsed her plate off, and went out the kitchen door just as the whooping cranes were coming through the dining room.

Both of them quieted down as they came into the kitchen. Mean Buck was squinting back another belly laugh so hard he was turning pinker than usual.

"Another delicious meal, Miss Butterworth. Unparalleled cooking. I'm deeply indebted to you for making my return home such a pleasure. And, Buck," said Thornton, as he clapped Mean Buck on his hammy shoulders, "another giddy, delirious evening."

He looked around, probably for Lily, and seemed to notice me for the first time that evening.

"Artie," he said. "Artie, Artie, Artie." He tilted my chin up so he could stare down into my eyes. I gave it back to him, peering into those dark eyes, into his shifty smile.

"My lad, are you still aspiring to join the ranks of the inspired scribes? Become my protégé?"

Before I could figure that out, Billie said, "A writer, Artie. Do you still want to be a writer?"

"No," I said. "I want to be a drag racer."

"No longer want to carve the great sentence of your life into immortal Kentucky limestone?"

Too much brandy. His bony face was crimped. There was a smudged smile on his lips now.

"I want to drive funny cars," I said. I did. I had taken a job at a local repair shop where I was hoping to discover the secrets of souping engines.

"Ah well, it is probably best. The world of literature is not the noble hall some imagine it to be. It can be torturous and mean. To make more than a measly living, one must pawn his very soul. It is only through the most scrupulous self-discipline that I have managed to stay untainted my-self."

"I'm saving up to buy a Chevrolet three-eighty-five short block," I said.

"Lofty," he said. "Lofty goal, my lad." And then he pat-ted me on the head like he might have done to a dog or a thirteen-year-old.

He stood at the kitchen door winding his scarf around his throat. He and Mean Buck exchanged one more clamped-back belly laugh, and Thornton screwed on his red felt beret. He'd picked it up somewhere in his travels and wore it nonstop, to funerals or fishing. There was some secret story to that hat that only Mean Buck knew. They'd flaunt it at supper sometimes, pretending it was so good that it might drive us insane if we heard it. I never once wanted to hear it, though. How good could a story about a hat be?

"Viva Miami Beach," Thornton said as he waved to us and pushed out into the cold night.

"Wonderful man," said Mean Buck, a little later, as we watched Thornton drive out our long dark driveway. "And I consider it a blessing that he finds this household worthy of his interest. I just wish all the denizens of this house could bring themselves to give him the respect he's due."

"Don't start talking like the boy," Billie Butterworth said.

"I talk the way I talk," he said, and moved away from the darkened window, where I could see Thornton's taillights turning out onto Hollow Road.

"When that boy has been visiting here, you take on his affectations so quick I think there's two Thornton Blandings for a minute. But there couldn't be two. There's not enough presumptuousness in the world to spread that far."

"What's presumptuousness?" I asked as we followed Mean Buck into the living room.

"It means she don't like Thornton a damn," said Mean Buck. "Which just mystifies the hell out of me. That boy gives all the credit in the world for his success as a writer to your mama, even dedicates his books to her, I understand. That boy'll tell anybody who'll listen that your mother showed him the road to art, to the whole vast world of beauty, opened his eyes like a surgeon slitting away cataracts. He's full of praise for your mama, Artie. But does she return an ounce of affection? No, sir. I'm sorry to report she don't. And Thornton Blanding is trying his damnedest to put us on the map. Put us on it big."

"And you're going to take us right off it, if you aren't careful," said Billie Butterworth.

Mean Buck sat down in his big padded recliner, leaned it way back, and muscled up one of those heavy books from the stack of them beside his chair. It was something about one utopia or another. Not that Mean Buck was a bit religious. He'd as soon drive away a Bible thumper as spit, but he was always reading those books. I'd see him every night of the week, asleep in that chair with one of those books lying like a dead eagle open on his chest.

The next day was Monday. I lay in bed and watched the second hand hum around. I watched it go around from five-fifteen till five-thirty, imagining it was some broken propeller on a plane that wouldn't ever fly. If I watched it hard enough, I could make it go so slow that I'd get an extra hour in bed. But the trouble was, I had to stay awake and work so hard keeping it from going around that it almost wasn't worth being in bed.

I flicked on my crystal radio and put the earplug in, and I lay back and listened to Mean Buck give the hog prices. Buck was mayor of Sinking Fork, and he also owned the only radio station anywhere around. You could listen to other stations, of course, but WOHO was the loudest, and lots of times you'd be listening to some station in Nashville or Bowling Green and here would come WOHO bleeding its way into your other station, quiet at first, then second by second getting louder till it finally crowded out that other station altogether.

Between being mayor and running WOHO, Mean Buck always seemed to get his way. There didn't seem to be anybody in Sinking Fork who could stare him down or who could hang on to the other end of a scrap of meat or a piece of bone that he wanted. No one but maybe Billie Butterworth. He'd get to wanting something and allowing as how it was the thing he wanted most in all the world and talking to anybody he met about this thing he wanted until everybody else was saying, "Get it, Buck, do it, Buck, go on, Buck, have that thing."

It might have been nothing more than a new collection of books for the library or a swing set for the park or new cheerleader dresses. But he'd moan and whine and then all at once be quieter about it than any man you'd ever seen. He'd sulk around, acting like it was just eating him away not to have that thing. And someone would come up to where he was moping about in the poolroom and he'd pull out his wallet and say, "Buck, get them cheerleaders the dresses you want." And everybody in the poolroom would go "whew." He just knew how to want things so much better than anybody else that it made you start to think that Mean Buck deserved everything he got.

When Mean Buck had finished with the hog prices that Monday morning and he'd said a word or two about what a raw, mean March day it was about to be, he dropped his voice down into a croon and started in on Miami Beach. He said how he had in front of him a half dozen postcards that people had sent him over the years, all of them from Miami Beach. Now wasn't that peculiar?

"I just want to describe these here photographs for you, help you wake up in a good frame of mind," he cooed. "This first one is of a row of buildings so white you'd think they were made of ground-up angels. And over the top of them you look out at the warm, lazy blue Atlantic Ocean, where the sun is just now coming up for another glorious day. The sky is awful pink, and there are flamingos floating in from some unspoiled offshore island and they're just gliding along on a sea breeze, salty and brackish, and they don't even have to flap a wing. It's a lazy, lazy place, Miami Beach."

He made his voice go low and soft like he was trying to convince a young girl to do something she'd always regret. He didn't let any spaces get in between his sentences, just hummed along like an auctioneer in slow motion, drowsing in the warm bath of his fantasy.

I curled my toes hard and gritted my fists, squinched my face tight, but it got to me anyway. I started picturing the summery easiness, the pink buildings with shady patios, the huge white birds on their stalky legs standing out in every yard, the perfume of tropical fruits and red blossoms, yellow blooms as big as women's hats, everything drenched and ripened by a sunny, lush bounteousness that was caused by the place being named Miami Beach.

I didn't have to do any of the work either. All I had to do

was close my eyes and fall into the lull and sway of his voice, and he described it, every lazy insect gone fat on nectar, every splash and slide of ocean coming ashore.

"Miami Beach, Kentucky," he said, wooing us all, all in our beds, all of us half-dazed from dreaming. "Miami Beach, Kentucky," he whispered. "We can make our town anything we got the gumption to imagine. All it is is like good Billie Butterworth always is saying, all life is is whatever you can imagine it to be. If you imagine it good enough, it's there. No one is forcing us to live with a shriveled-up sense of our lives. We can have the Garden of Eden, pure and simple, if we can imagine it hard enough."

Then he went on about palm trees and ferns and lobsters and crabs and egrets and laughing gulls, sandpipers and marlin, dolphin, sailfish, red snapper, sea turtles, tarpon. Everything had a charmed echo to it like something you'd wished for years and years before that suddenly was coming true. Waterfalls, sand dunes, shrimp, rum drinks, suntans, bathing suits, sandals, sea oats, gardenias, toucans, grouper, wahoo, cockatoos.

I floated in a cool green current, drawn ahead into a rush of cooler, greener, clear waters, and I was gliding into a sort of drunken happiness when Billie Butterworth yanked out my earplug and snapped me all of a god-awful sudden to raw, gray, stubbly Sinking Fork, Kentucky, where out my window the branches of the Chinese elm were clacking together in a gray wind.

"He's doing it again, isn't he?" she said.

"This is a good one."

"They're all good ones."

"This one could work, I'm thinking."

"They all could work," she said. "Except that nobody can

wear an earplug every minute of the day." She let my earplug drop on the bedside table.

She was dressed for school already. A brown wool dress with a high collar. I was thinking more along the lines of my shirt with the hula girls on it.

"You lie there till you get your brain back, boy. Then get on to breakfast." She held my hands for a minute and looked at my eyes like a referee checking out a boxer after he's been down.

I lay there and let the surf noises die down. I squirmed and listened to her walking downstairs, trusting me not to plug up again.

For years Mean Buck had been dreaming up schemes which were going to save Sinking Fork from itself. Not that there was any thread running through all the gimmicks. Every year or so he'd catch some new sickness and the town wouldn't have a blink of rest until Mean Buck had squeezed every recollection, every date, snatch of gossip, folklore, family tree from every single citizen so that Sinking Fork could have the most complete historical record and genealogy of any town in America. Next time you'd caught your breath, Mean Buck would be heating up again and in your face claiming that each and every Sinking Forker should donate ten percent of his income so we could once and for all get rid of poverty. I don't know how much he squeezed out of the town on that one, but it was enough to buy new suits and dresses for all eight of the Negro families who lived in a little shanty town out by the graveyard. And it was enough to buy them all bus tickets to Los Angeles.

There was kissing and hugging at the bus depot that morning as white people lost their lifelong nannies and maids and gardeners, and the high school band was there to play, and lots of flash pictures were taken. Mean Buck gave each of them a wad of bills, right down to the little ones in their Easter clothes, and they all smiled and waved at us and got on that bus and waved and smiled till the bus disappeared. So we all stood around and listened to the band play for the rest of the morning. And I heard one or two people ask Mean Buck, "Why Los Angeles?" And all he could tell them was that if they'd had a better idea, where'd it been when the choosing was going on?

So Sinking Fork didn't have a poor problem anymore, and we had the greatest genealogy records anywhere, and we had a football team with uniforms made in France or somewhere and a lake on the edge of town churning with more fish than could've survived in a lake five times as big.

The one just before Miami Beach was still on everybody's mind, I imagined. It was his there-ain't-nothing-out-there-we-can't-bring-in-here campaign. It had started off a year or two earlier, when a few families had got tired of it all and moved off to Nashville or Shady Grove. Mean Buck had called an emergency town meeting and explained how Sinking Fork was glad to get rid of those faithless bastards and how Sinking Fork was just like America had once been, a great big experiment that required all of us to spend damn near all our waking hours figuring ways to keep it all bright and new and alive. And how it was cowardly and un-American to leave the town where God had had the good sense to drop you, cowardly and shameful to drift off searching for some cheap satisfactions. It was one of his speeches that had whiskey in it, that made everybody, even the old women in their berry-covered hats, stand up and wolf-whistle and cheer till the turned-up basketball goals in that auditorium swayed.

He had some of us children walk up and down the aisles, taking up all the suggestions of what to bring to Sinking Fork to make the town a cultural paradise. I was swollen up with pride, my shirt tight against my chest, thinking how I was blessed to be the son of such a mover and saint. I took the wad of papers and dropped it beside his feet, and he leaned down and mussed my hair and split his cheeks smiling out at the wonderful, lucky citizens of Sinking Fork.

A couple of days later the *Sinking Fork Reporter* printed up a list of the most popular suggestions. Miss America was number one with seven votes, and five people wanted to bring in some blond Hollywood actress I hadn't heard of. Four people had asked to see a pig with three heads, and there were a couple votes each for a giant squash collection, a seven-hundred-pound wrestler, the Mormon Choir, John Dillinger's weapon, a pygmy, and the horse that came in fourth at that year's Kentucky Derby. I heard that Mr. Mosley and his wife requested that so they could shoot the old nag for losing them so much money. My suggestion didn't get into the paper. I wanted to invite Little Daddy Crawdaddy to drive his double V-8 dragster at the Sinking Fork airstrip.

Mean Buck was awful disappointed with the suggestions, but he told everybody on his morning radio show that he was going to do his damnedest to get Miss America at least, and maybe even that squash collection. It was about six months later when Miss America showed up. She'd won the thing about fifty years before and could barely walk anymore, but she wandered around town for a couple of days, smiling and shaking everybody's hand and saying how happy she was that people hadn't forgotten her, and she made everybody feel so sorry for her that I didn't hear anybody complain that she wasn't that year's Miss America. But if Mean Buck thought she was liable to keep anybody else from moving away from Sinking Fork, he was wrong. Five more families moved out the week after the squash collection arrived.

I lay there in my cold bed for another five minutes till I could feel the proper chill for a March day. Then I got up, dragged myself in and out of the bathroom, and went downstairs, where Lily and Billie Butterworth were dangling their spoons into the steam from their oatmeal, and watched the steam fog over a purple brooch Billie wore on her wool dress.

"Why does he do this?" Lily asked. She kept staring at her spoon, which she held like a mirror in front of her face.

"It's the way he's built. He has to do it."

"Why don't you make him stop? You could if you wanted."

"I know it's embarrassing for you two. And it's never been easy for me either. But I tried once to stop him from this, and I saw then that if I'd won and I'd got him to give up all this foolishness, it would've been like I snatched his heart right out from his chest. The man has never been any other way. He gets an idea how to make the world a little more interesting, and that just crowds out every other thing in the man's mind."

"Including his common sense," said Lily.

"I don't see how calling it Miami Beach is so bad," I said.

"You wouldn't, half-wit." Lily put down her spoon and changed her eyes on me, turning them a sickening yellow, the color of a withered-up skink.

"Changing the name is just the beginning of something bigger, I'm afraid," said Billie.

"You should've gone on and ripped his heart right out of his chest," Lily said, her eyes still shiny yellow. "You might've donated it to somebody who could've used it proper."

"He's your father," Billie said, like she wasn't sure.

"I don't have one," she said. "I ain't got any use for fathers."

We drove to school in the Falcon, Billie's car. She'd bought it a few years before so she could drive out into the countryside and paint cows and barns and streams and meadows. When she'd painted every barn and cow and every single tree within a day's drive of Sinking Fork and filled up the basement with her rolled-up canvases, she'd slowed down a whole lot, gotten moody. It was one of the reasons I was trying to learn to soup up engines. I guessed that if I could get the Falcon to do over sixty, Billie could get out that little bit farther where the sights were new, out where there were cows she'd never seen, and maybe she'd cheer up and start painting again.

When we parked in the gravel lot, Lily stalked off one way and Billie went on up to her office. She was principal of Sinking Fork High, which might've made it rough on me if she'd been some kind of maniac paddler or rule follower. But she wasn't. She treated everybody, even the punks and hoods, like they were her children and like all of us were on some kind of leaky boat in the middle of the ocean and we had to stick together if any of us had a lick of a chance. I was glad she didn't make it hard on the punks and hoods, 'cause mostly they were who I hung out with. It wasn't that I didn't like the creased pants crowd. I didn't mind them, their clubs and church groups and dance parties. I might've even liked them if they'd known a thing about cars. They didn't. It was just the punks and hoods who knew about cars.

Most of the hoods had old Buicks and Chevy jalopies that needed work all the time. And they'd all hang out near school, in a parking lot near to Dunn's Grocery, where there'd be two or three of them every morning, getting greasy in their engines. Somebody might be rebuilding a carburetor or putting in a new timing chain, and there'd be spark plugs and wrenches and sockets lying all around, and somebody would be playing the radio loud, and all of them would be smoking and cussing and talking about some hot rod or other they'd seen come through town, something bright yellow with flame decals coming off the front wheel wells and black furry dice hanging from the ceiling, with lake pipes, street slicks, moon hubs, no hood chrome, rolled and pleated Naugahyde, rhinestone mud flaps, and a thirty-degree rake.

"A nigger car with no guts," somebody'd say.

"I could take that car in reverse, man."

"If you had a goddamn reverse."

There'd be haw-hawing and a little recreational punching maybe. But mainly they'd talk cars. Fast ones and pretty ones, street metal that was likely to overheat if you drove it under eighty-five.

But on that Friday, as I came around the side of the shop building, I didn't hear any hawing or anybody's engine racing, no squealing tires or loud radio.

I stepped out of the cold shade into a patch of halfhearted sunshine, and there they were, all of them hunkered on their bumpers and their hoods, some even sitting up on their roofs. Black jackets zipped up, cigarettes dangling, all of them looking on as Peggy Belle Brewster sluiced up her thighs with coconut butter. She sat on a Confederate flag beach towel, wearing nothing but her red bikini, and there was no guessing about what she was oiling herself with 'cause the air was practically edible with coconut smell.

Peggy Belle's father owned the only car dealership in town, so she already had aroused more than average notice among the hot rod hoods. And lately, as her sweaters had begun to throw bigger and bigger shadows, she had become the only other subject out there in the parking lot aside from fuel injection and the like.

Peggy Belle was down to her wiggly toes, oiling up each one with so much care it looked like she might spend her morning on just one foot. Her legs were shining, and drops of oil on her stomach lit up like fish scales. It was hard to know where to look and what to look for.

Speed Covington, the oldest and meanest of the car hoods, swooned as Peggy Belle oiled up her big right toe. He slid down the windshield of his '39 Packard, his arms wide open, moaning under his breath. He kept on sliding until he came over the right fender and sprawled in a panting heap a yard or two from Peggy Belle's blanket.

As she finished her right foot and moved slowly up that leg, I heard the first-period bell ring. By the time she'd finished doing her shoulders and the firm meat of her upper arms, the bell for second period had rung and two more of the hoods had fallen off their cars and lay like wreck victims on the ground near Peggy Belle. The others made swallowing sounds and groveling noises.

It couldn't have been much above freezing, but she didn't look a bit cold, and I was pretty sure that none of the rest of us were either. Her eyes were as blank as someone just saved by a traveling preacher, and I knew that Mean Buck's cooing voice must have been sloshing around inside her still. There were always a few of them like Peggy Belle who slipped in early and deep when Mean Buck had a fresh idea. And you'd see them on the street or at the grocery humming whatever tune he'd hummed into them or breathing with his rhythm, smiling silly.

And you could always spot the other kind, too, the ones who knew better than to wake up with their radios on and let Mean Buck have a free shot at their muddled brains. They'd be the ones gritting their faces, looking nervous this way and that, like they were stalking a housefly, more careful and shivery than seemed good for a person. They'd hang back from whatever it was Mean Buck had decided was good for them, and they'd talk to nobody.

But he'd wear them down eventually. Either they finally turned on WOHO 'cause they knew they'd never sleep or have a second's easy breathing until they'd at least heard what he had to say, or else they'd simply march up to Mean Buck's office in the courthouse and demand to have it out. More than a few times I'd been there and had seen Mean Buck smooth down a jumpy one, talk and smile, joke and croon. And before they'd leave that office, they'd be saying, "Yes, sir, I knew it was a good idea for everybody to learn to talk French, but I just was a little confused as to why."

"*Au revoir,*" Mean Buck would say.

I watched Peggy Belle Brewster oil herself silly until finally Billie Butterworth came back to the lot, probably having smelled the coconut butter in the wind. It was noon by then, and we'd drawn a little crowd. The football coach was there, a deliveryman for Sinking Fork Dairy, the school janitor, the butcher from across at Dunn's Grocery, and half a dozen stray dogs. When Billie cleared her throat, the dogs broke for home and Coach Thurgood hunched over and tried to hide inside his baseball cap.

"You people go find where you left your brains," she

said. "If you look hard, you might find what's left of them."

I went over to her and touched the sleeve of her wool dress. She drew her arm away and studied me for a minute.

"You got your brain back?"

"Yes, ma'am."

"Sure it's all yours?"

"Yes, ma'am."

We stood there looking at each other for a while in that uninterested sunlight. Her hair was primer black, and it hung long and heavy down her shoulders. Her eyes were as tough and blue as faded denim, and they could sometimes be as soft. If she wore makeup, I never saw her put it on and it didn't show. Nothing could have softened her features anyway, short of sandblasting. All the bones in her face made impressions. Her eyebrows were squirrel-colored and thick. And there was always a smile on her lips that was just a bit painful-looking as though somebody had just confessed to being scared of butterflies.

"Miss Billie?" It was Peggy Belle, wrapped up in her Confederate blanket, looking purplish and weak now.

"Girl, I don't want to hear a word of what you got to say. I heard it all before. I hear it in my sleep."

"It's this Miami Beach thing. . . ."

"Peggy Belle Brewster, you find yourself a bar of soap and wash off that gunk and put your clothes back on and get in there and learn something useful. And tomorrow morning when your alarm goes off, you don't even consider turning on the radio."

"Yes, ma'am."

When Peggy Belle had edged away, shivering, Billie regarded me again.

"You've got some of his blood," she said finally.

46

"Yes, ma'am." It was true. I could feel it in me sometimes.

"And you got some of mine. And that means you're going to have God's own awful time telling loony from true. A harder time than even the average dizwitty in this town." She put her arm around my shoulder and steered me back toward the high school. "I been spending so much time with Lily, helping her tell which from what, that I just hadn't given you enough thought."

"I'm all right."

"Are you?"

Nobody in his right mind could have answered her yes. Especially somebody who was Mean Buck's son.

"I'm not for sure."

"We'll get this straight," she said. "Somehow."

I got through school that day by counting up the Florida shirts and Bermuda shorts and sandals and whatnot. Billie might've sent them all home for dressing so crazy, but that wasn't how she went about things. I counted five parrot shirts and two hula girl shirts by homeroom. And I got three more parrots, a green tropical island shirt, and four Bermudas and four sundresses the rest of the afternoon. By the time school was out all of them were shivering and chattering and hugging themselves 'cause Billie Butterworth had cut the furnace way down low to remind all of them where they were and what part of the year it really was. That's how she worked.

I had kept thinking about that blood in me and how every other corpuscle of it was liking all the summertime clothes, was grinning and feeling warm, while the in-between corpuscles were sneering and embarrassed, wobbling with shame for the mush-headed human race.

After school I walked down to Al's Garage, where I worked. I just wanted to set timing or grind a camshaft and not think about any of it anymore. But the minute I stepped inside that cold, greasy building, I could hear Mean Buck's voice on the radio, making love to whoever'd listen. Miami Beach love. Sand and warm breezes, the thrash of surf, a freshwater swimming pool for every child and woman and man, shuffleboard, sailing, deep-sea fishing, mangoes and grapefruit and coconuts, orange blossoms pumping out their sugary perfume.

Big Al and Little Al were sitting in the waiting room. Both of them wore their blue overalls, and Little Al held his crescent wrench. Neither of them looked up when I came in.

"Pink fish, pink shrimp, pink houses, pink flamingos, pink sunrise, pink ocean at sunset, pink skin, pink hibiscus."

Big Al was staring up at the speaker in the ceiling like he'd heard someone whispering his name. Little Al beat on his leg with a wrench in time with Mean Buck's speech. I felt those corpuscles going at it in my legs. They quivered to go, but I stayed.

"Balmy moonlight, saxophone and rum, a slow dance beneath a canopy of stars, deck chairs in front of the phosphorescent sea, the rattle of palm fronds, the gardenia-drenched night, hot damn, what a place!"

"What is it he's wanting from us this time, Artie?" Big Al asked me, his eyes still struck numb from so much radio jabber.

"It ain't any of my business," I said. I took a grip on the doorframe and pulled myself away from his voice. When I got to the doorway and stuck my head outside for some rough, honest Kentucky air, I felt those other corpuscles squealing, trying to lock the brakes on me. They held me there and let Mean Buck work on me some more, but then those other ones nudged me toward the sidewalk. I felt a splitting rip of lightning fire through me. There was one last "boat ride across a rolling meadow of moonlight," and I was free.

Thornton Blanding was at supper that night, and he amused himself and Mean Buck by telling tales about famous cities he'd been to. He was holding up the clown glass half full of beer and describing a bullfight he'd seen in Madrid where the bull had refused to go charging at the cape. No amount of slapping or whistling, clapping, or name-calling would make the bull run. And when finally the matador came around behind the animal and struck him an awful blow with the side of his sword on his rump, the bull let go of a mountain of shit and covered the matador from slippers to sequins. Mean Buck sputtered, then coughed up a laugh that trembled the table.

They crowed and blustered for near to five minutes over it. All the while Lily was putting her eyes through ninety-nine colors. She glared mostly at me like she was daring me to so much as smile, but when she turned on Mean Buck and Thornton, her eyes turned as blue-white as a welding torch.

"Have you ever seen anything in your travels for which you have the slightest respect?" Billie asked Thornton when the laughing had died down.

Mean Buck kindled his laughing up again, probably thinking he was saving Thornton from an embarrassing question.

"It's not the job of a writer to respect things, Miss Butterworth. I have only to observe and report."

"But you've seen nothing out there that you love or admire or care about?"

"That's not the point," he said. He held my clown glass up then. "I would like to propose a toast."

Mean Buck cleared his throat and stood up beside Thornton.

"To the person who elicits from me the greatest measure of respect, love, admiration, and all the other eternal emotions, Miss Billie Butterworth."

"No, thanks," she said as she stood up and began clearing away the pork chop remains. "I don't have any desire to appear on your rating system."

"How high did the shit actually get?" asked Mean Buck.

Thornton drank the last of his beer and saluted Billie's back with his empty glass. "Up to his cravat," he told Mean Buck.

"Up to his neck in shit!" He trumpeted out another laugh.

Thornton joined him then, and they were still sputtering when the back door barged open. A cold swish of wind blew the napkins off the counter, and into the kitchen stepped Mrs. Edith Sherwood, the librarian at the public library and the granddaughter of the only Confederate general from those parts. I'd never heard of her breaking into people's kitchens before.

She stood there for a second getting her bearings. On her white hair she wore a gray and beaten-up forest ranger's hat. And as usual, she had on long wool pants and a sailor's blue jacket.

"You men stand up. There's a lady here," she said as she pulled off her leather gloves.

We all stood up, Thornton smiling cockeyed and Mean

Buck red-faced. Billie asked Mrs. Sherwood if she wanted to sit down and have some leftover cobbler and some coffee with us.

"I came to give a speech," she said. "I don't sit down with the enemy."

"Artie, you and Lily go on and get your homework done. You can be excused."

"The children stay," Mrs. Sherwood said. "Isn't anyone in the household excluded from what I'm about to say."

"You children stay," Mean Buck said right away after her. "You might learn something."

Thornton was grinning like a moron in mud.

"How are we the enemy?" asked Billie.

"Don't be coy with an old fox. I haven't gone senile just yet," she said. "You better sit down, too, Billie Butterworth. I've got a harangue here, burning." She patted her breast. "And if I don't get it out now, I may just have to strangle someone instead."

Billie took her seat, and we all settled in.

"Harangue away," Thornton said.

She began to pace between the stove and refrigerator. She was so gaunt she might have been feeding on bobby pins. Her mouth made a clicking noise like she was fiddling with her dentures. She paced and paced with her hands behind her back, and Mean Buck started to grumble, watching her careful.

"I own a radio," she said, finally coming to a stop. "Some fool gave it to me for a present. But I never learned to listen to it, and I'm awful glad of that. I haven't ever had a yearning to have someone's voice, who I wouldn't let through the front door, come crawling into my room, all over me and my things. I never felt any feverish desire to hear someone guess about the weather when it's right outside the window to see. And what they're calling music this year, I'm calling turkey squeals. But I've got some old lady friends who aren't so ornery, and they get lonely and dreamy and want to have somebody talking to them at all hours of the night or day. And it's them that brought me the news of this . . . this . . ." She waved her hands around in the air, drawing some kind of pantomime monstrosity.

She cleared her throat and straightened her forest ranger hat. "I'm proud to say that I have opposed the folly of your various intrigues in the past. I have willingly borne the label of 'malcontent.' I am not a simpleton, sir. I'm not the sort easily seduced by nonsense.

"Today your latest campaign was described to me by friends of mine who *can* hear the radio, and I have come here tonight to declare war on you and your clan until you drop this outrageous plan to steal the birthright of those of us who have our roots in Sinking Fork."

"Now, now, now," said Thornton. "I must disagree with you, Mrs. Sherwood. Renaming towns in American is not outrageous or even very unusual. I think your obsessive preoccupation with the past is muddling your thinking on this issue."

"And you call yourself a writer."

"Yes, ma'am. I most humbly do," Thornton said, straight back at her. He touched his goatee then.

"And he's a famous one," chimed in Mean Buck. "Whose books fill a whole shelf."

"Not in my library, they don't."

She paraded between the refrigerator and stove again, huffing and slapping her gloves against her open hand. Mean Buck pushed his chair back and stood up, his face a Florida sunset.

"I'm flabbergasted, Mrs. Sherwood. An intelligent woman like yourself, someone holding the public's trust, admitting to hiding Mr. Blanding's books from undernourished minds. I believe we may have us a First Amendment violation here."

"I don't hide them. I burn them."

Some gas went out of Thornton's smile, but he held on to a last tatter of it.

"I don't believe a mayor in my position can tolerate such a thing."

"Pshaw," she said at him. "Billie, how could you go on for all these years putting up with a frog-faced weasel like this? Have you lost every ounce of your Noble gristle?"

Major Willard Noble would have been my granddaddy if he hadn't been killed in a tractor accident.

Billie Butterworth didn't have an answer for her. It could have saved me a whole god-awful lot of time if she'd just said right there how someone with blood so different from Mean Buck's could stay around him so long.

"Is it just the marriage bonds? 'Cause if that's all that's keeping you caged here, I can speak to Judge Dyer tomorrow, and snap, like that, you'd have cooked this rascal's last good meal."

"We can't have no librarians burning no books," said Mean Buck, like he was landing in the conversation for the first time. You could see his heartbeat in his face. Blue earthworms dug for cover in his forehead. He was standing so close to Mrs. Sherwood that he might have been about to pin a medal on her coat.

"I want to know what you're up to with this Miami Beach insanity."

"I'm not in the habit of discussing my political goals with

former librarians." She held her ground as he leaned toward her, and you could have toasted marshmallows in the air around them.

"You tell me here and now what you're up to or I'll go out in my car and get General Sherwood's long rifle and ventilate that runty little head of yours."

"A death threat?" said Thornton, raising his eyebrows. You could see him scribbling away behind his eyes.

"I don't have nothing more in mind than unburdening all of us of a name that makes us sound like a passel of hayseeds. People don't believe we discovered electricity yet when they hear that name Sinking Fork."

"A real writer would know this is wrong," she said to Thornton. "A true artistic writer respects the past and tries to create in harmony with those pure authentic verities that spring up throughout history. A real writer shows no interest in the trivial and empty baubles of his time. He's too busy arm-wrestling with the gods."

Thornton just stared at her like she was a talking burro.

"I intend to sweep all this hick town nonsense away," said Mean Buck. "I'm bringing us into the twentieth century. Making us the jewel of Kentucky, the bright pink beauty of the South. I intend to move beyond the mere dabbling I've been doing and correct the whopsided interest in farming and what not around here and make this town the paradise on earth it was meant to be."

"It was meant to be a widening in the road, and that's all."

"No, ma'am. I fully disagree."

"Buck," said Thornton, "this woman has made a public threat on your life. I feel we should advise the authorities of this immediately. A man in your position can't take lightly the possibility of assassination."

He seemed to hear Thornton, but it didn't settle in. "I plan to rewrite history, not follow it. I plan to correct the nincompoopism that's been the way here for so long. I got a way. There ain't nothing I'm not going to change about this town. Nothing, not even the weather."

"You're a madman," she said to his blustery face. "The weather!"

"She means to kill you, Buck," said Thornton.

"Yes, I expect I should call Dan Overfleet, Sheriff Overfleet."

Mrs. Edith Sherwood hauled back and slapped Buck once, twice, three times. And then got in a fourth one before Thornton caught her hand.

"Wake up, you old fool," she shouted at him.

"Help me with this bone bag, Buck," Thornton said. But Mrs. Sherwood wouldn't be held. She twisted loose, shook her dignity back into place, and marched out the back door. Thornton asked Mean Buck if he would be kind enough to offer him a shot of whiskey, and Mean Buck led him off to the library.

We must've sat there for another ten minutes, digesting it all. It got so quiet you could hear that big house creaking and moaning like an old man asleep. I didn't dare look across at Lily 'cause I knew she'd have her eyes racing. It came to me then that maybe it was possible that I had nothing but Mean Buck's blood in me and that Lily was all Billie's blood. We'd split it in half. It gave me the willies thinking like that, and something in my stomach went dizzy. I started picturing it, how it wasn't really red like blood was meant to be, like Billie's was, but something with froth in it, something weak-eyed and whitish. Pink blood.

I reached out across the table and picked up my clown glass and poured out the last of Thornton's beer onto my dinner plate and slung that glass across the kitchen over Billie's head at the back door. I took that look at Lily then. And just as quick I wished I hadn't 'cause her eyes were unplugged. Still green like normal, but there wasn't a fleck of light, a bubble of fizz still in them.

"I'm sorry," I said. For the glass. About her eyes. My blood.

"It's the least you could do," said Billie. She stood up then and went over to the coat peg by the back door, crunching through that glass. She took down her coat and put it on and took down Lily's and mine, too. "Come on, let's get."

"Get where?" I asked her.

"Come on, Lily," said Billie. But Lily didn't wink, didn't breathe. "Come on, girl. It'll be all right."

"It won't ever be all right till you oppose him, make him stop. You just let him grab that old lady and never said a word. You never say a word that does any good."

"I'm a painter, not a doer," said Billie. "Least, not lately. I've about forgotten how to do."

"You hadn't been painting either. At least Mean Buck's got some life. I hate him, but he's got some life in him."

"You like him so much, go tell him you'll be his head hula girl," I said.

"Leave her," Billie told me. "She's got to handle all this her own way."

I got into my coat and followed Billie Butterworth outside. She walked over to her Falcon parked in the driveway under a pear tree. Cold night, the air clean, no grass smells, not even woodsmoke, just the bright, empty sting of frost.

She got behind the wheel and cranked it up. The fine

whine was still there from a tune-up and carburetor adjust-ment I'd done on it earlier that month. I slid in beside her and watched the Hurst tach I'd installed on the steering column. The needle rose and fell as Billie pumped the gas.

"Where we going?"

"Where you want to go?"

"California."

"Why?"

"It's where Little Daddy Crawdaddy is." He was abso-lute king of speed. Pro stocks, funny cars, jet dragsters, top fuelers, and anything with wheels.

"So you go there."

"You're not coming there, too?"

"We don't have to go the same place."

She revved up the Falcon then, 3500 rpm, and held it there, steady, and I thought she was going to pop the clutch and go screaming, fishtailing down the driveway. But she didn't touch the clutch and she held on to that steering wheel like it was Mean Buck's throat and she looked out into that dark, cold night.

Five minutes, ten. I got fidgety.

"What's going on?" I called to her over the racket.

She didn't answer me but kept her eyes on the driveway ahead of her, giving the wheel little nudges and pulls like she was darting in and out of slow traffic.

I looked out at the stars. They seemed to be all there. I'd always meant to learn the names of them, learn how to read the road maps I'd heard were printed up there. I watched one faint one for a while, pretending we were really on a trip somewhere, just Billie and me, and it was up to me to keep us steered right. She drove on, and I kept watching that star I didn't know the name of until some water clouded over my eyes from eyestrain and some of it ran cold down my cheek and my nose got runny. I had to give up pretending I knew where we were and let Billie just drive.

A long way later I fell asleep, my head bumping against the window. The last thing I remembered was that pear tree swaying a little like a drunk late at night.

Then I was awake again. And there was frost on the side window and the heater was on, keeping the front windshield clean, and Mean Buck was hammering on the hood of the car with his fist. Billie held it at 3500, and Mean Buck whammed away at the hood. When that got nowhere, he came huffing around to my door.

"Let me in, Artie."

I wouldn't look at him.

"I'll break this goddamn window."

But I knew he wouldn't.

He thumped on my window with his knuckles until they must have hurt him. The engine churned on. Hot oil and rubber smells were coming through the floorboards. Billie was bulling ahead into the darkness. Going somewhere she had to get to. Mean Buck came around and stood in the headlights again and put his hands on the hips of his trousers and panted like a horse.

"Throw her in gear, woman. Go on! Run me down!"

I thought I felt the engine nudge up a notch. He screamed at her to run him over now instead of humiliating him into the grave. When that didn't faze her, he came out of the headlights and stood next to her window and yelled that he wouldn't fire Mrs. Sherwood and he'd think twice about this Miami Beach thing, though he did say he still thought it was the best idea he'd ever had. Then he slapped his open palm on the windshield in front of her a few times, but she didn't flinch. It seemed to be no more to her than smearing a bug at fifty miles an hour.

Finally Mean Buck slouched off. The engine drove on. I woke up a little before daylight, and the tach was still hovering at 3500. I listened for any dings or sputters or one of those little coughs Big Al had taught me signaled carburetor clogging somewhere later on. Nothing doing. It purred perfect and the sun came on out and it all warmed up a few degrees.

It was maybe nine-thirty on that Saturday morning when Mean Buck came outside with Lily and got into the Lincoln and sped off. Neither of them glanced over to see us, and I felt spooky like maybe we had actually disappeared onto some road that only Billie knew the way to.

I played around with that for a while, pretending to myself we were on some straight, straight highway that shot directly toward California, a wide endless drag strip with Little Daddy Crawdaddy waiting at the finish line. I imagined what we might be seeing out there beyond the Sinking Fork city limits, beyond Kentucky even, heading west, dipping down from mountains, skimming across bridges that looked down on huge rivers or canyons and zooming through frontier towns lit up with neon and reflective signs and flying out across prairies and deserts, past cactus, sagebrush, tumbleweed. And then it was like getting to the second verse of a Christmas carol and not knowing any more words but still having the tune singing away in your head and going on and faking the words but really just mumbling: tumbleweed, cactus, sagebrush, mountains, deserts, prairies, ghost towns, valleys.

I sat there dead and awake. Listening to the engine,

knowing I could never keep up with Billie Butterworth, with how far she could burrow inside herself. I was just there, in that cold front seat, watching the pear tree shiver, watching sparrows jitter around on the phone wires, hoping she'd bob back to the surface soon.

It was Sunday afternoon before that Falcon ran out of gas. I'd peed out the door twice and nearly gnawed off the fake green leather from the dashboard to have something to chew on. And I'd had dreams I wasn't sure were dreams and pains I wasn't sure were pains.

As the car sputtered and slurped the last of the gasoline, Billie began to loosen up the frown that had set like a plaster mask on her face. She softened up into a smile and sniffed once or twice the way she might to test a casserole of squash. Then she was back.

"Well, we got to get us a bigger gas tank next time," she said.

"We'd make better time if you'd of put it in gear."

"We did all right. It was fine to be away, wasn't it?"

"I didn't go much of anywhere, I don't think."

She glanced over at me then, and her eyes took back some of the sadness she'd left behind on the drive.

"I see that," she said. "We're a little different, is all."

"Who?"

"All of us. You from me."

"I think my blood's pink."

"You're different, is all it is. And I'm different."

I opened the car door then, and smack, it hit me right off. It was a huge amount warmer out there, and there was some kind of flowery honey in the breeze, something like the smell of coconut flowers or hot sand or something I didn't have anything close to a name for.

Out of the back door came Lily. She had her arm around
Thornton's waist. As they walked over to the car, to where
Billie was out limbering up, touching her toes, taking deep
breaths, I saw Lily's eyes. They were green and smiling.
But it wasn't any smile you'd ever dream about. It was the
way a butcher smiles, all peaceful and happy, talking to
you across the meat counter while he hacks away at some
carcass.

"Come around front, y'all," she sang out, and started off
down the driveway, that arm still slung around Thornton
Blanding.

"Welcome back," he called over his shoulder. He waved
his red beret at us. His arm was around her shoulders.

"We were away too long," I said. "We should've stayed
here and kept a better watch on him."

Billie just sighed.

Around front we stopped beside Lily and him on the
edge of the terrace. And there was Mean Buck, wearing a
pair of white overalls, up on a scaffold, putting the last
swipes of turquoise paint on the top of the last of eight
columns on the house. They'd been white. And the red
brick wasn't red anymore either. It was rusty pink, the color
of the inside of a fish's mouth.

The air was swarming with new smells. Not just spring
smells either. They weren't any Kentucky smells. Fishy,
fruity, salty smells.

"I love it," Thornton called up to Buck. "It's superb."

"Hello, Mother," said Lily, still inside Thornton's arm.
"You're looking rested."

She didn't answer. She was staring at a white bird standing out on the terrace. It had long orange stems for legs and
a warped black beak. She made a run at the creature, clap-

THE
ELECTRIC
POET

The Electric Poet arrived at the Famous Writers Conference at one-thirty in the morning. There was only one light on on the front porch of the inn, and since he had no idea what immense panoramas might open up come daylight, he decided to recline his front seat, parked where he was, just off the road. It was important to him not to be caught sleeping by anyone at the Famous Writers Conference.

Unfortunately his trip from Florida had exhausted him more than he'd thought, and in the morning what woke him was not the New England sun on his face but the hubbub of voices around his car. A face, in fact, was planted in his window. A man in a crew sweater and herringbone coat, clearly a writer, breathing fog from the summer morning chill, was trying to get the Electric Poet's attention, without actually speaking or rapping on the window.

"You'll have to move your car," he said finally when the Electric Poet had opened his eyes.

The poet rolled down his electric window and erected his seat at once.

"You'll have to back up very carefully," said the writer in the coat. "You are astraddle the Robert Frost Flower Plot."

"A flower plot," said the Electric Poet.

Glaring at the Electric Poet through the windshield was a young blond woman in a tartan overshirt. Her fists were on her hips.

"I'd say half the bluebells are done in," came a voice from under the car. "If the joker came straight back, we might have a shot at saving the white heal-alls. He got the birch sapling, too."

"Oh, no," said somebody nearby.

The Electric Poet started his station wagon and waited for instructions. There were perhaps twenty people on the porch of the inn by then, watching silently. The writer in the coat had replaced the blond woman at the head of the car. He motioned the Electric Poet to back up. When the moist crunch of the wheels came, a wince circulated.

"Hold it, hold it!" The Director of the Famous Conference appeared on the porch. He barged past a couple of nuns, apologized briefly, and suddenly was in the seat beside the Electric Poet. He thought the Director was much puffier than the photographs on his book jackets made him appear. This was not how he had pictured their first meeting either. The Electric Poet shut off the engine out of respect.

"What the hell do you mean by plowing up this flower

bed! Some of these flowers are ancestors of ones Frost himself planted three decades ago. Robert Frost. Know the one
I mean?"

Bacon was in the air. The Famous Director was over-
weight. Must be fuming because of the delayed breakfast.
So much fuss over a lot of spring flowers. Poets!

"Shall I back up?"

"I don't give a good goddamn." The Famous Director
was somewhere else, seemed to be holding a conversation
with someone who'd done him dirty. The Electric Poet
didn't let it bother him.

"I respect your poetry," he said. "I drove up here from
North Miami Beach so I could let you experience mine."
Then he told the Famous Director his name.

"Oh, joy." The Famous Director grimaced at the Electric
Poet and looked him over with heavy-lidded dismay.

Sleeping in his car hadn't done much for the Electric
Poet's ice-cream suit which was already brightly stained
from leaky tacos in North Carolina and New Jersey. Cer-
tainly his new ponytail was loose. He was within ten years of
being the Famous Director's age.

It was then that the Electric Poet's beeper began to
screech.

Before he could explain to the Famous Director that he
was picking up someone's maternity call frequency, the director had hopped out and stalked back up past the nuns
and the woodsily dressed others.

"Not a good opening," he said to his roommate, a Writing Teacher from Texas. The Electric Poet was hefting the
echoplex out from the rear of his station wagon.

"Say," said the Writing Teacher, stacking an oscilloscope

carefully on the back of an Advent speaker, "just what is an Electric Poet anyway?"

"It is"—the Electric Poet paused and stared into space— "it is the next step."

The seminar on prose poetry was evenly split. The young men in collegiate glasses and young women in men's clothes claimed that prose poetry was the possible redemption of the innate artifice of the poetic tradition, and the old codgers, who by now were sitting together and were paying close to seven hundred dollars for two weeks of this, half of which went to pay scholarships for the college people across the room, the codgers believed that any airhead could write prose, and why were they in a seminar on poetry if they didn't care to write real poetry, and if they were prose writers, they should just admit it and shut the hell up, and then there were the staffers and Famous Writers themselves who had stirred up the discussion to begin with so they could sit back quietly and get over their hangovers, and who didn't give a rat's ass one way or the other. The Electric Poet sat in the front row and was gazing out the French doors at a pretty girl playing croquet on the green.

He was listening to every word and mincing them all in his imagination. Rendering them harmless, returning them to the alphabet. Prose. P.Rose. Pro's. Pro sss. Oooooossssee. P. P. P.

"Why do you wear a beeper?" whispered one of the nuns, who was not included in the three just-mentioned categories and really had no interest in such hairsplitting and was attending the Famous Writers Conference for a few laughs and the view.

"In case I'm needed," said the Electric Poet.

"Who would need you?"
"You never know till you get one of these things."

At the end of the first week the Electric Poet met with the Famous Director in the barn. Converted into a rustic conversation hall and bar, the barn had once housed some Belgian draft horses belonging to a friend of Robert Frost. History everywhere.

The meeting between student and staff member of student's choice was regarded as the highlight of the conference and a large part of what one came up with seven hundred dollars for. The Famous Director was shuffling a deck of cards, reshuffling them, quarter slicing them, and evening their edges as the Electric Poet approached. It was one o'clock. The Electric Poet hoped the director had eaten a hearty lunch.

Out of respect for the Famous Director's legendary skill with cards, the Electric Poet did not speak. He found himself splintering words again. Barn barn. Bar. N. Bar none. Baron. Rawbone. Bare on. Ba Ba room.

He sat down in a leather sling chair and scooted it across the wood floor a yard, so he was elbow to knee with the director. Cards shuffled. Cards fanned. Conversations were occurring all around them. Other conferences. The dark-haired Ethereal Woman Poet was holding a sheaf of poems written by a Frail Young Man, and she seemed, as she talked unflinchingly to him, to be trembling with mystical enthusiam.

"Shall we begin?" asked the Electric Poet when the cards had come to a momentary rest.

The Famous Director resumed his maneuvers with the cards.

"I have read all your work," the Electric Poet said. "Several times. Even the *Pachyderm Sonnets,* which I had to pay dearly for. I was told you were the best living American poet. And you used to be."

No reaction from the Famous Director. More shuffling.

"Your best poems were written when you were twenty-five. And your new book is all cant and bombast. It's a sad display. But you know all this. When you were twenty-five, you were drunk on your sap's rising. You knew more than you knew. And now, now that you do know those things, you don't have the excitement to write them down."

He waited for that to register. Just more shuffling.

Zing. Zzzz ing. Ning Ning Ning. G. G. GeeZZZ.

"I saw that coming in my life. I was a program analyst for a sugar futures outfit. And I saw it heading my way. I was at the top and bored and coasting. I started looking around, and I tell you, I was scared. I didn't want to end up teaching. Teaching some twenty-five-year-old in a week what it took me all my born life to learn. In a hurry for retirement so they wouldn't find out I hadn't done a new thing in forty years.

"I wanted a new profession, something with class and something creative. And I wanted to be able to make a splash in it. You can't splash unless you're in a quiet pond. I found it. It was American literature.

"I ask you, what's doing? I ask you honestly. Go into a supermarket and ask a checker about poetry, and she'll say chicken is the best buy this week. Look around this place. American literature needs me, just like it used to need you.

"See, your best work is over and mine's just arriving. I'm in touch with the new technology and you're still Gutenberging along. I've seen how the next big splash in American literature is going to come. I'm there, on the cutting edge."

"Electric," said the Famous Director. "Electric poetry." He'd stopped shuffling.

"Right."

"What do you want from me?"

"Keys. The keys."

"Do that again."

"Keys to the kingdom."

The Famous Director tried to laugh. It didn't work, sounded like phlegm realigning.

"Come hear me tonight."

"Oh, I plan to."

"You will be astonished. Astounded."

"Undoubtedly."

"I need money."

"Who doesn't?"

"It's gotten too expensive. The equipment. Every new poem costs me plenty. Sometimes several thousand. My savings are drying up. I need a grant. Large bucks."

"And I can snap my fingers . . ."

The Electric Poet put his hand on the Famous Director's knee.

"I want the Nobel Prize. Literature. Or I'd settle for Peace."

"You're mad."

"Just a nomination. I can do the rest."

The Frail Young Man nearby was making an announcement. He was standing on a side table and speaking to the entire barn.

"Please, please!" He clapped his white hands together. "I want to buy all the drinks. All of them on me." The

Ethereal Poet, more voraciously prolific than anyone at the conference, anyone in North America, stood beside him, beaming at anything.

After the Electric Poet's performance there was a gathering in the barn. Everything had gone well with the show, except a strobe had blown out in the opening poem and a fuse in one of the feedback modulators had gone. When he stepped into the cheery light of the barn, a Wizened Novelist blocked his way immediately.

"Disgraceful," he declared. "Unforgivable."

"Aroused you, did it? Made the old blood zip. That must be poetry then."

"That's puke," said the Wizened Novelist.

The Famous Director was sitting before the hearty fire, laughing at something said by the Jewish Lesbian Poet from California. A couple of young women stood nearby, smiling, sipping from paper cups. The Electric Poet stepped into the charmed halo, and all the smiles shut down.

"Well?" he asked the Famous Director. "Have you recovered yet?"

The director beseeched the rafters and said nothing.

Using her talk show drawl, the Jewish Lesbian Poet said, "I believe I have recovered."

The Famous Director was resting his eyes now. A painful doze.

"It was somewhat silly, don't you think? Jejune," she said to the Electric Poet. "Like an adolescent disc jockey having a seizure. Somewhat embarrassing to witness."

"Or Mick Jagger without rhythm," offered one of the young women.

"I thought it was gauche," said her sidekick.

"Bosh!" exploded the Famous Director. "It was magnificent. The most amazing and disciplined concoction I have ever witnessed. You, sir, are in a pasture by yourself."

"Horseshit," said the Jewish Lesbian Poet from California.

"Thank you, sir. You mean it. I can tell." He squatted down between the Famous Director and the fire.

"Of course, he doesn't mean it, unless old age has finally jellied his mind."

"I mean it," he said. "And you, you are going to be quashed by this. You and all your simpering, smug, mumbler friends."

"Transistor trickery. Blue-collar male paranoia bullshit."

"I want you to give a performance next semester at my Famous Northeastern Elite University."

The woman poet snorted.

"For five thousand plus travel," said the Famous Director.

She stalked away at that, her two friends following at a distance.

Two friends. Twooo friends. Tooof rends.

"And that is my entire budget for readings or I would offer you more."

The Electric Poet stood up and took a confident pose in the chair beside the Famous Director.

There was a fleck of mirth in the director's eye.

"You think my show is ridiculous, don't you?"

"Utterly grotesque. A scurrilous parody of art. And you are a repugnant cretin."

"But you think we can put it over, don't you?"

"I can shove it down their throats, yes. I think I will enjoy shoving it down deep into their throats."

He looked over at the Jewish Lesbian Poet from California, who was gesticulating at the Raffish Drunk Novelist from Montana, pointing back at him and the Famous Director.

"Then it's a deal," said the Electric Poet. "We're going to cram me down their throats."

"Deal," said the Famous Director.

SURVIVAL
WEEK

The evening my letter came from Chief, advising me of my selection to Camp Tsali, my father gave me a grim smile of approval and led me down to his woodworking shop in the cold basement. He opened a panel I had never seen in the side of his workbench and withdrew an old compass.

"This will be yours now," he said, using that tone he reserved for ominous rites of passage. "This will be your first attempt at swimming," he had said years earlier in the same grave way as I stood trembling on the lakeshore.

He handed me the compass and I nodded.

He drew on his sawing goggles, leaving the lenses up against his forehead while he continued to regard me with detachment. It was as if he stood on one ridgeline and I were on the next one over. We seemed so close, yet there was a twenty-year valley between us. I would have to hike miles of broken, intricate terrain before I could see the view he saw.

I peeked at the old compass. It was rusted and had a feathery crack across the dial. Down there in the basement among all my father's tools and heavy metal equipment, it probably wasn't indicating true north.

"Of course, you must learn to navigate by the stars," he said, "but this compass was your granddaddy's when he attended Camp Tsali, and it helped me get through Survival Week there, too. All the Connor men have used it, so I knew you'd be touched to have it."

"I am," I said. I held it up and watched the needle wiggle.

He kept studying me as if for flaws. And the kitchen was quiet above us, where I suspected my mother and younger brother were sitting silently, staring into their cleaned plates, participating from afar in this ritual.

"This would be an appropriate time to ask me questions about anything that's bothering you."

"What?"

"Mysteries," he said. "The sex issue. Things of that sort."

"Chief explained it all pretty good," I said. "Siamese twins. Superfecundation, all the diseases. I think I've got it down pretty good."

"Siamese twins."

"And superfecundation," I repeated, for he seemed puzzled.

"All these things are important, yes."

I had heard Chief give the Sex Talk seven times in the

seven summers I had attended Camp Wind and Arrow. I had repeated whole passages of it like Scripture whenever some baffling new heat stirred inside me.

"Son," my father said, "Chief will want to make you into a man. Are you ready for that, to become a man?"

"I'd like to be one," I said. "I want to be one."

"When you come back, you'll be different."

"I'm ready to be different," I said.

He secured his goggles then, and he aimed a hairy plank of cedar down the runway of his saw and stepped on the starter. I waited around until the first shriek had become a savage whine, until his hair was dusted with wood flakes and his mouth had gritted into the noise and fray of particles. And I drifted away toward the stairs.

The first ceremonial fire of the summer was built by Woodrow, a college by and former Tsaliman whom Chief had selected to be our leader for the summer. He was a knobby boy, all gristle, with pale blue eyes that seemed to swivel perpetually, on the lookout for rebellion, irony, contempt.

Woodrow chipped flint against steel in the dark before us. When finally the fire had begun to settle in and hiss and spit, Woodrow moved away from it and Chief rose. He opened his arms wide, arched his back into a swan dive stretch, and gazed at the sky, which was white with stars.

"Welcome to Camp Tsali."

Some of us murmured. He lowered his arms slowly.

"By now you have all seen the Camp Tsali motto carved into the lintel at the entrance of camp. Some of your fathers helped carve it there. 'Will the boy you were respect the man you become?' He paused.

I had already gotten a little lost in the syntactical time warp of the motto, but I leaned back against the dew-damp bench and savored the moment, readying myself to take flight with him.

He looked magnificent that night. A large man, unstooped by his seventy-nine years. He wore his usual uniform of khaki pants, red plaid flannel shirt, work boots. Most of us were dressed similarly. He had a healthy red face and a thick tuft of white hair. His eyes were even paler blue than Woodrow's, and in the twisting light of the fire they seemed to be filled with a juicy brilliance like the glowing centers of grapes.

"I selected each of you carefully, from the hundreds who pass before me every summer at Camp Wind and Arrow. I've selected you to become Tsalimen because I saw in each of you a deep hunger."

That was it, I told myself. That was what I felt, a hunger. I watched Chief gaze deep into that fire. I said that word, *hunger,* to myself. Grateful finally to have a name for the feeling.

Chief spoke toward the fire. "Women," he said. "Women are not like us."

From somewhere in the circle of Tsalimen I thought I heard a soft chuckling.

"Women are the other half, the half which draws us away from a life of discipline, hard work, power, strength, steel blue purity. They are soft, wild, passionate animals. They drink of our strength, grow bold on our attention, rob us of power. They undermine our true mission.

"You have all heard me in previous summers describe the diseases that result from sexual adventurism, the debauchery that can overtake an unwary young man. I've pro-

vided you with tools to survive in a sexual world. Now, in
the coming weeks, I will reveal to you a higher doctrine
than mere survival. I want you to flourish, not merely survive.

"Ask yourself if you can flourish if you waste your bodily
fluids, your strength, in pursuit of fleeting sexual satisfac-
tion. Ask yourself if you want more than the lives your
fathers have settled for, a life debased by a woman's insatiable appetites."

Chief looked up at the sky again, and the dark, cold night
air danced down our necks.

"Will the boy you are become a man who succumbs?"

"Say no," said Woodrow impatiently.

"No," we all mumbled, out of sync.

"Will the boy you are defile the man you become?"

"No." We got it better that time.

"Will you surrender to the shallow, phantom pleasures of
profligacy?"

"No!" There was one "yes" in that chorus. I was aghast. I
peered around for the guilty one. Chief, however, seemed
not to have heard.

"I know that what I am proposing to each of you is
beyond any challenge you have ever imagined." He
searched the unraveling fire for several moments. And then
he looked at each of us in turn. "Will you accept my challenge?" he asked, a quaver in his voice. "Is there even one
among you who can muster the courage to let your natural
chastity grow into lifelong purity? To shun Delilah forever?" He looked sadly around our group. I felt myself
shrink as his eyes touched mine. When he'd completed the
round, he sighed. "Go now," he said, quietly. "Hold back
your voracious and savage desires. Hold yourself under

tightest rein, walk carefully, measure every breath."

The dark rose up all around us as we marched silently back to camp. Only a small path of light left from the dying campfire and a single lantern hanging in the latrine guided us.

Before we broke up to our cabins that night, we milled around in the latrine. I stood before one of the urinals, waiting for something to happen. The others brushed their teeth quietly or simply studied themselves in the small metal mirrors nailed to the walls.

"He's bonkers," I heard Cox, my cabinmate, say.

"You can't talk about Chief like that," said Dupree, a baseball player from Louisiana. "He's Chief."

"Chief of the loonies," said Cox. "Chief wacko."

"Who *is* this guy!" someone else asked.

"Cox," I said, over my shoulder.

"I heard from my brother that he's been giving that same talk for about thirty years," said Thurston.

"He's been doing all the same things for thirty years. That's tradition."

"That's senility," said Cox.

"He wants us to be men," I said. "He's trying to change us into men."

"Well, let's get on with it, get to it," Cox said. He was a tall, thin boy with large ears and a pointy chin. There was thick black hair showing at his cuffs and at the brim of his undershirt. His eyes were sunken and shadowy, and his lips were thin. One of his eyebrows was cocked in a permanent "did-I-hear-you-right?" look.

"OK, who is this dipstick?" Thurston said. "I never saw you at Wind and Arrow. How'd you get in here?"

"His old man must've made a donation to camp," someone said.

"Hey, Cox. You getting a hankering to succumb?"

"Hilarious," said Cox. "I can see why the old fellow is so worried about you boys spreading your seed."

I left for the cabin then. Between being assigned Cox as a cabinmate and hearing Chief's talk, I was a little low. I was also thinking about how I was going to break the celibacy news to Mae Beazley.

Mae Beazley. If I hadn't been falling into my bunk bed at Camp Tsali at that moment, I would have been kissing Mae Beazley on the seventeenth green. Nothing beyond kissing, but we still managed to dizzy ourselves from that.

Blond hair, skin that tanned wonderfully from hours by the Country Club pool. Blue eyes and a small dark mole on her left cheek. I believe, though, it was the Country Club connection that made her irresistible. My family didn't belong.

For the last few months Mae had been losing patience with me. When we were out on the putting greens, warming ourselves with kisses, she'd begun guiding my hand to new and scary parts of her.

I had told her, "Mae, I'm not sure about this touching."

"You don't need to go to camp to learn to be a man," she had said.

"I don't want to be that kind of man."

She said, "There's only just two kinds I know about. Kind that like to touch me there. And you."

"There was a young man from Nantucket," recited Cox from the doorway of our cabin.

I dug deeper into my sleeping bag as he filled the wretched air with his rhyme.

In those first weeks of camp Chief devoted the ceremonial fires to Kahlil Gibran and Norman Vincent Peale and

Psalms. And he found abstinence and holiness intertwined in every passage. Each night the fire was lit by another of us, and every night, as Chief stood up to address us, I listened carefully for any escape clause, any hedge on his opening remarks. But nothing came. Chastity stood before us, rising like Mount Mitchell into the clouds, and Chief stood at the first switchback, hailing us upward.

Cox and I divided our cabin exactly in half. On the shelves above my bunk I laid out my cache of survival tools: water-purifying tablets, a collapsing plastic cup and bowl, high-protein pills, waterproof matches, my grandfather's compass, three flashlights and spare batteries, insect repellent, a whetstone, a Swiss Army knife the size of a baked potato, a twenty-foot nylon rope, a book on birds, one on edible plants, a novel I had to read for my senior year in high school, and a book of modern poetry.

Mae Beazley wanted me to write a poem for her.

Cox's shelf was bare. How he expected to survive Survival Week without any equipment was beyond me.

Survival Week was at the heart of Camp Tsali. It was what we were all in training for. It was to be the fifth and final week of camp. Woodrow would lead us far into woods none of us had ever seen, and one by one we would be left behind. We were expected to find our way back to Tsali, feeding off the land for seven days before we entered camp.

One night, about midway through the summer, as I was working on that poem for Mae Beazley, I glanced across at Cox, who was lying atop his tangle of sheets, staring at the rafters.

I was trying to write the poem in such a way that it told Mae that I liked her a lot and had enjoyed kissing her a great deal, but that now a new force had entered my life and I would have to break up with her. It always came out sounding as though I'd found somebody else who kissed better.

"You've never been in love, have you, Cox?"

"My answer is to provide tomorrow's amusement?"

"I'm serious."

He stared at me for a minute.

"No. The answer to your question is no."

"I didn't think so."

"And neither have you."

"You can't know that, goatface."

"The condition, as I understand it, requires more emotional maturity than you have. A person cannot truly experience a great many important events in his life until the proper emotional or psychological foundation has been laid."

"You mean I won't know for twenty years if I loved her or not?"

"It's like that," he said.

"What good is an idea like that?" I remember snorting at him.

We hiked for twenty miles with packs full of rocks. We built lean-tos and then tore them down. Hauled fallen trees that winter storms had left blocking the trails. Repaired the lookout tower, collected boulders, and with them built a chimney and hearth for Chief's Tsali cabin. We studied map reading, star reading. We gathered plants we believed were edible, and with Woodrow smiling and shaking his head, we ate them.

We climbed thirty-foot ropes and slid back down. We ran

up steep trails carrying small logs. We did calisthenics in a clearing of poplars and maples each morning and then sprinted to breakfast.

Every night I lay in my bunk and pretended to sleep until Cox rose and dressed in the dark and sneaked out of the cabin. He was always there when I woke in the morning, and despite many attempts, I could not stay awake to see how late he returned. I supposed he had walked down the mountain to the office phone at Camp Wind and Arrow and had called home or called a hideous girl friend who I imagined wore a frayed black turtleneck and had a voice like a kazoo.

And every night when he had gone, I focused my mind on my hairless chest and tried to raise my blood pressure to the heights required to force the black curly hairs from their caves. Hair had appeared already in the crucial zones, so it was not a matter of grave embarrassment for me to shower with the others. But chest hair was the true glory, one of the things I had imagined I would acquire at camp. I had also expected to develop man strength that summer, a condition, according to locker-room lore, in which the muscles suddenly developed the tensile strength of armor and my boyish suppleness would be forever gone.

Each morning, when I woke, I would lie in my bunk listening to the catbirds call, running my fingertips across my sternum, probing for the first soft twirl of hair and then squeezing my tightened biceps to see if the steel had filled them overnight.

My turn to light the ceremonial fire came the night before Survival Week. One lucky spark from my flint landed on a thin curl of wood and caught. It was a triumph. I moved back to my seat beaming.

"I married a woman," Chief began that night. "I was not celibate. I even produced an offspring in a moment of hedonistic surrender. But for sixty years I have followed the path of restraint that I have described for you, and I owe all my greatest achievements to it."

Chief said, "In this group tonight, I sense there is one of you who wants more than anything else to be free of earthly passions, the tomfoolery of romance, the chimera of love. There is one here who knows what this summer offers and is ready to choose. Up into heaven or down into the grave of insatiable cravings. Up or down."

"In and out," whispered Cox.

I heard the soft thunk of someone striking him.

"Only one of you will be allowed to return to Camp Tsali. Only one of you will solve the riddle of Survival Week and take over for Woodrow next summer. Who will it be, who!"

"Holy blue balls," hissed Cox, "let it be me." And again the thunk.

"Tomorrow begins Survival Week," Chief intoned. "These, then, are your final moments of boyhood."

His voice still thrilled me, as it had down the mountain when I was just an innocent softball player, a lanyard lacer, a maker of wood-burned plaques for my mother. I felt the old confidence, the familiar heart-swelling anticipation. His talks for so many years had made my life seem exceptional. For days after one of them, every trivial action was freighted with fateful consequences.

Somewhere between tree felling and constellation naming, I had decided to pledge my future to Chief's vision, accept an austerity beyond reason. I was prepared to sacrifice sex. I was ready to give up what I had never known and what I half feared knowing. Monks did it, priests, men who were not insane. I was prepared to do whatever it took to be a member of Chief's family of saints. To hell with Cox and his sneers. To hell with his slouching and smirking and naysaying. I would tell Mae Beazley straight out, no poem, no pretty excuses. What were these flesh and bones for if not for some higher purpose? Did I want a life of aiming cedar planks down the runways of saws so that my mother might have a new picnic table? Wasn't a man diminished by the constant womanliness he must endure in a marriage?

Chief gazed at the streaming sparks, following them up to where they winked out and became the white flecks of stars.

"Tomorrow you will enter the forest. You will each become some sort of man this week. It is up to you to decide what kind of man you want to be: one that the boy you were will respect, or one that you would loathe.

"Believe me, if you can weather this week, your life of chastity hereafter will be easy. Your potency will decline rapidly after this, your seventeenth year, and that part of you which lusts for the creamy center of a woman will wane and wither, dwindle, and drop away."

"Like his," said Cox.

Woodrow led us at a very fast pace over Bald Knob into the national park wilderness area, a region we had never hiked before. We followed no trail, and we twisted and circled so many times that I thought for a while we must be headed back to camp. We covered maybe fifteen miles by lunch, and in the afternoon we were dropped off in alphabetical order a mile or so apart.

When the group had marched away and I was alone with my pack, listening for the last traces of their chuffing, I began suddenly to fear for my life. I had no food, only three matches, a length of rope, my Swiss Army knife and water-purifying tablets. I had the echo of Chief's voice. And I had the consolation of only two lonesome hairs, which had appeared that week on my chest.

I looked around me at the plants. I saw nothing I could name. My panic had swallowed every skill I thought I'd acquired. Utterly blank, I stared at my compass. It wavered, pointing this way, then that as if the years had finally worn away its magnetism.

I headed back down the ridge I was on, following a vague trail. But when it separated into three paths, I faltered. I sat on a rock near the intersection and felt the hot flush of panic, the burn of tears rise inside me. I had a week alone. Even if I had known the way back faultlessly, I would still have to dally, for it was as inglorious to return early as to become lost. And to dally in my condition was probably to starve.

As I sat there, I thought I could hear sounds from Camp Wind and Arrow, the smack of a baseball bat and the faint cheering that followed it. The bugle calls, reveille and taps, the iron dinner bell. All of it seemed to come floating up from the valley like the lyrics to sad songs I had almost forgotten. For a moment I thought I could simply follow those pleasant noises and be back, perhaps even camp on the outskirts of Wind and Arrow until the day I was permitted to reenter camp. But even in my clouded state I knew it was only an hallucination. Wind and Arrow was at least fifteen miles away. I fought off the fantasy and made myself listen to what was truly there, only the soft scrabblings of the woods.

For an hour during the midday heat I stared out at the distant ridges, those mountains whose trails I had hiked for

years, and I wondered who that boy was, why he had labored so, what had called him up those peaks. As I sat
before that panorama, a powerful craving woke in my belly,
a greater hunger than I had ever known.

When the noise of something moving through the brush
came, I was tasting the first salty trickle of my tears. My
sinuses opened instantly, and I stood. Bears, I thought. I
was trembling when Cox tapped on my shoulder.

"Musing on a little Kahlil Gibran?"

It was a full minute before I could summon the breath to
answer him. He watched me with an expression I had never
seen on his face before. Though I would never have been
able to give it a name then, I see now it was something close
to tenderness.

"I thought you were a bear."

He smiled at me and started down the ridge, and I followed him. A serious transgression in Survival Week law,
for we were supposed to be alone, the solitude no less of a
test for our skills than any of the rest of it.

In a short while he came across an old log slide, a slick
grooved trail lined with stumps that ran down the mountain
by the steepest route. The pull of the slope brought us both
to a stumbling run in a few yards, and we continued to run,
dodging fallen branches, our fifty-pound packs pushing us
faster and faster down the incline.

And then the land leveled and greened, and we were
suddenly in knee-high grass in a field that sloped down toward a small farmhouse. And in the field were apple trees,
and three women in white dresses standing on wooden ladders, picking the apples. And at one side of the orchard was
an old man sitting in a metal wheelchair watching the
women.

I followed Cox over to the man.

"Coxy," said the man in the hill twang of that region.

"Hubert," Cox replied. "This is Connors."

The old man nodded at me, gripping the lapels of his frayed robe with one skinny hand as if against a sudden chill. The man's skin was yellow, his eyes drained of color, and the hair that showed around the edges of his Red Man cap was whitened and brittle as spun glass.

"Hubert's got the cancer," Cox said to me.

"I do indeed," he said.

"I'm sorry," I said.

"Posh!" the old man grumbled. He held me earnestly with one blurry eye. "I keep telling Evelyn that now I get to see how it is to have a baby growing inside."

I nodded.

"Same exact thing, I say. This tumor thing growing, it's you, but it's not you. It's hurting you, but in a way you got to love the damn thing, tough little son of a bitch. And as soon as the thing gets big enough, well, then you're all over, you don't count for beans forever afterwards. It turns you inside out. Changes everything. Same exact thing as having a kid."

Cox said, "I best take a look at the damn machine, Hubert."

Watching me intensely, Hubert said, "But then Evelyn, she allows as how having a baby is a marvel, what comes of love. A miracle and a revelation. That it's just a man's jealous pride makes him want to claim something that can equal what she can do easily.

"Know what I say back to her?"

"No, sir," I said.

"I say, how did an amoeba get to be a man? Think he just

sprouted a couple of legs and hopped up and started fussing with bridges and radios? No, sir. There were stages. Steps, one by one. Evolutionary stages. And these tumor things, they's the steps to whatever's next. And if we can't see what it's going to be, and we look at this step and say, 'God Almighty, this is one horrible creature,' then we're just plain shortsighted. That's what I tell her.''

"I'm getting to that machine now, Hubert," Cox said.

"Say hidey to Mercy Ann first now. Don't pretend on us, Coxy.''

We set our packs down beside Hubert's wheelchair, and I followed Cox over to the orchard. From their ladders the women watched us approach. Two teenage girls and their mother. All with wheat-blond hair, freckled faces, and eyes that shone green as the leaves of those trees.

Cox introduced me to them all. Mercy Ann, Joy Beth, and the mother, Evelyn.

The mother asked if I knew anything about machinery.

"Next to nothing," I said.

"That hasn't stopped Coxy," Mercy Ann said.

She climbed down the ladder, and as the other two resumed filling their straw baskets with the small apples, she took Cox's hand, and the three of us walked down an aisle between the trees and came to the long, rusty contraption that I came to know in that week as the Washer.

It was Hubert's invention, a long table with a corrugated rubber belt running down the middle of it, and scrub brushes attached to metal arms suspended from overhead and shower heads aimed down at where the apples were intended to be passing by. It looked even to my unmechanical eye like the stupidest, most roundabout way to do a simple thing that I'd ever come across.

"Maybe I could pick," I said as we approached the machine. "I don't think I'll be much help with this thing."

Mercy Ann smiled at Cox, and Cox shook his head at me.

"Take a month to train you to pick," he said.

"I picked apples before. Good grief."

But I had never picked them correctly. Mercy Ann took me over to some gnarled trees in the far corner of the orchard, the practice trees, she called them, and there I showed how little I knew of breaking the apple free of its branch. There was a twist, a slight turn and pull that broke the connection in the cleanest way, avoiding any damage to the branch and insuring a good crop the following year. I tried a dozen apples, and my tears were ragged and left a snarl of wood fibers where Mercy Ann's broke free as if sliced with a razor.

"Machinery," she said, halting the lesson. "That's all you're ready for."

That night we pitched our tents on the edge of the orchard and we made a fire and Mercy Ann and Joy Beth brought out some stew they'd made and we ate it off tin plates, quietly watching the fire. In the house they were playing the Victrola, some Italian tenor with a voice that shook my blood.

Joy Beth was a couple of years younger than I was, but when Mercy Ann and Cox went for a walk into the dark orchard, she asked me if I wanted to kiss her.

"I got a girl," I said.

"One's all you allow yourself?"

"Look, I'm in a lot of trouble," I said. "I'm not supposed to be doing any of this, being here, talking to you all. I'm supposed to be out in the woods, alone."

"What in the world for?"

"Becoming a man," I said, but it sounded awful silly, especially saying it to a fifteen-year-old girl. "It's a trial, an ordeal. Like Jesus in the wilderness."

"Jesus wasn't any man," she said.

"What're you talking about?" From the house came more singing, this time it was Evelyn singing "Silent Night," Hubert's croaking voice coming in on the refrain.

I said, "That what they teach you in your backwoods school? Jesus was a girl?"

She said, "Jesus was the strongest person in the world, wasn't he?"

"Yeah, OK?"

"But when they came to take him off, he let them. He let them spit on him, whip him, punch him, call him awful names."

"So?"

"A man around here would spit back at 'em, oyster for oyster. They'd fight and push and cuss. Wouldn't you? Wouldn't any man? Isn't that what a man does?"

So I kissed her.

And she kissed back. Not at all like Mae Beazley. But making her mouth fit mine, going soft, making mine go limber, too. Until our faces were melted, tongues dancing together. And I wasn't there anymore. And not worried either. Not worried for the first time in a very long time. I wasn't thinking, weighing, deliberating. I wasn't trying to decide which way to send my life. I was kissing this fifteen-year-old girl out in a cold, dewy August field with her parents singing Christmas songs a few yards away.

Cox and I spent the next day trying to disassemble the Briggs and Stratton motor that was supposed to power The Washer. Every bolt was rusted, every gear frozen into

place, but we budged and cranked and twisted and got a few
of them loose. It was maybe four o'clock when the girls
came over to us in cutoffs and T-shirts, Joy Beth carrying a
Louisville Slugger.

"Want to hit some homers?"

"Sure," I said.

They led Cox and me over to a field of clover that sloped
down toward a stream. They let me bat first, Joy Beth pitch-
ing and Mercy Ann in the outfield and Cox catching. She let
fly a crab apple, hard and green, and it came in a slow arc
and I took a good cut at it anyway, turned it to applesauce
on that bat.

"OK," I said, laughing along with the others. "Now let's
get serious."

"All they use is apples," Cox said to me quietly.

So I creamed a few more, the bat a sticky mess by then.

"Let Cox show you," Joy Beth called.

And Cox took the bat from me, wiped it in the grass, and
took a stiff unathletic stance. He sent the first crab apple past
first base, only a fragment breaking off, and he hit the next
two over Joy Beth's head into short center field.

"How do you *do* that?" I said.

"They'll show you," Cox said.

I pitched to Joy Beth and then to Mercy Ann, and every
apple I threw they homered into the stream beyond the
field. I even threw overhanded, rifling it down the strike
zone, and whoosh, over my head, over Cox's head, in one
piece they sailed to the stream, some even to the bank
beyond.

They tried to show me how it was done, how I was swinging too hard, whacking instead of whooshing. But every
apple I hit dissolved on the bat.

"He's a case," Joy Beth said as we stood around in the twilight, me holding the sticky bat.

"He's pretty far gone," Mercy Ann said.

"Even Cox caught on faster than this," said Joy Beth. "But I still think the boy's curable."

We stayed the week and never got the machine going, though Hubert said we'd gotten it a lot closer along to working than it had been. I'd gotten to where I could get that crab apple back to the pitcher's mound. It was coming to me. If Survival Week had only been two weeks, I might have made it.

I'd hitched my pack on and was standing there looking at them all when Joy Beth came over and gave me a long kiss right there in front of everybody and in daylight. And when it was done, everyone was smiling at me and Hubert had a tear on his cheek, but that might have been from the cancer. And even Cox had that look again. His face so relaxed, you'd never know a sneer had ever passed over it.

It took us about an hour to walk back to camp. And he and I walked under that motto together, not saying anything, but just walking back to the cabin and lying down on our separate bunks and taking a long nap until supper.

I was not changed. What had happened that week was still setting up in me, hardening into the shape my life would take. Only now do I bring back the silent mumblings of those first true kisses, the juicy whoosh of an apple against hard swinging wood.

For only now have I reached the ridge where my father stood. A place where I can call across the valley to that boy struggling up the paths, trying to be good and smart and true. I call out to him to tell him it is OK, to come ahead, he will survive this. Perhaps he can hear me; perhaps he calls back. But I can't be sure, for the valley makes echoes of our voices, sending them out and bringing them back, swirling together one with the other. I want to tell him that it is OK if he does not understand love. No one does. No one ever has. He will not either.

The tradition was that all five hundred boys from Wind and Arrow with their counselors would assemble along the roadside to watch the Tsalimen march down the mountain. We carried all our gear, for we were going home that day. Our parents waited in the outermost parking lots.

Some of us had grown beards. We were dirty, sweaty from the hike down. Rough and primitive and a little mean. The boys from Wind and Arrow watched us with fascination, as I had so many times watched.

Chief led the procession. The camp nurses were there, standing on the porch of the infirmary. The black cooks in their whitest uniforms waved washrags at us. One young cook beat time on the bottom of a huge kettle.

My father waited by the Nash. Mother was inside, busy with something in her lap. As Chief led one after another of us Tsalimen over to our fathers, the rest of us stood in a nervous cluster, telling each other farewell.

I found Cox at the back of the crowd and told him good-bye. He let me have a final look at his secret face.

"Chief chose me to return," he said. "Take Woodrow's place."

"Maybe you'll get that damn machine going then," I said.

"Doubt it. But I'll try."

I shook his hand, but we both knew that wasn't enough.

We embraced while some of the others watched.

It came my turn, and Chief led me across the parking lot. My father studied me as I approached.

"He's a young man now," Chief said as he shook my father's hand. "Ready for all the rest of it."

"I can see that," said my father.

We got into the Nash. My mother greeted me quietly. There was no kissing.

As we drove away down the long entrance road shaded by tall pine trees, my father said to me, "Chief seems to be younger than ever."

"The boys keep him young," my mother said.

"I think it's seeing the boys grow up," my father said. "The thrill of it. Right in front of his eyes."

"You know, Mae Beazley's been asking about you," said mother.

"The Beazleys are good people," said my father as we turned onto the main road.

"She's matured a good deal this summer, too," my mother said.

My father winked at me in the rearview mirror, and my mother saw him and gave him a playful swat.

"You know what I mean."

We headed east for a while, then turned north onto the parkway. My father's dashboard compass jiggled and kept up with all the twists in the road.

My mother reached across and laid her hand gently on my father's shoulder. I can still see him smiling in the rearview mirror.

ARABELLA

$\mathcal{T}$oward the end she had a battery-powered talking clock.
It was a gold cube with a large button on the top and a
speaker in the front. Arabella would wake and reach over to
the bedside table and press the button, and the clock would
speak the time in a voice that was a great deal like her dead
husband's.

In fact, Arabella had begun to think of the clock as the
dwelling place for her husband's ghost. Now that her eyes
had died, she relied almost totally on his voice to keep her
on course. Naturally it occurred to her that the clock might
not be completely accurate and that she might be rising at
ten at night to cook breakfast or she might be putting on her
nightgown and cleaning her dentures at ten in the morning.

And this bothered her a good deal. There was little enough else that kept her anchored to this earth anymore. Little enough else to trust.

She couldn't completely rely on her daughter-in-law, since it would be just like Cynthia to lie to her and tell her that the clock was correct when in fact, it was hours off. Cynthia might even go so far as to reset the clock to throw her off or perhaps even time one of her visits very late at night so that Arabella would be deceived into thinking it was morning.

Once a week Carmichael Junior would come along with Cynthia, and she could get an honest answer from him. But between his visits she was powerless against Cynthia's whims.

It was Arabella's fault, of course. If she'd had children of her own, she could be counting on them during this period. Her first husband had died before they'd been married six months, just long enough to steal her away from New Orleans and deposit her in this small Tennessee town, where she had stubbornly stayed.

Next she had married Marty Shots, the owner of the local Buick dealership and an extremely handsome and well-tailored man. But Marty Shots had been a homosexual, a fact which he had neglected to disclose to her before their marriage. So, while Marty followed the high school sports teams from season to season, going off on all the away games, the loudest and most charitable booster the Maryville Hornets ever had, Arabella remained at home and celibate. Her rose garden and fruit trees in summer and her book clubs and bridge parties in winter were her only distractions.

She'd married Carmichael when she was fifty. It had

taken that long for Marty Shots to be beaten to death by an all-state tackle and left in a ditch along the Mayfield Road.

After thirty more years with Carmichael, treating Carmichael Junior just like a son, here she was, a widow again. Though Carmichael Junior and Cynthia pretended she was a part of the family, they were clumsy actors. Whenever the family gathered, everyone always labored a little too hard to be gracious. Their smiles seemed printed up for the occasion. They nodded their heads in quick agreement to whatever outrageous thing Arabella said. "Green beans cause stomach cancer? I *do* believe there's something to that." "Red cars always drive faster? I believe I've noticed that myself."

Whenever Arabella got irritable and depressed the way she was at the moment, she told herself that it was the lack of birthing children that had done this to her. Her family's blood had made a wrong turn and was dammed up inside her, and all the love that had brought her ancestors together and had flowered into new shoots, endlessly reaching out into the future, had stopped inside the withered veins of her own body. She had loved two men, and it had come to nothing.

Lately the clock had begun small attempts at conversation. Arabella would carry the clock into the living room and set it beside her on the couch as she sat listening to the woodpeckers hammering on an old poplar tree outside the window. She had tapped the button just that afternoon, and the voice had said, "You remember Woodlake?"

Off she had gone to Woodlake, Florida, where Arabella and Carmichael had owned a beachfront condominium in the last years before he died.

"Of course, I do," she said. "I'm not batty."

The clock was silent.

She sat for a moment recollecting the pattern of their life at Woodlake. Every morning studying the dog racing forms over coffee, choosing a few long shots, selecting a few arresting names. Arabella chose dogs with floral names. Petulia's Folly because it sounded like petunia. Lucky Sucker because of honeysuckle. Carmichael chose them on the basis of numbers. Six, seven, and three were his lucky ones, and combinations of those or additions of them. He always made a few last-second choices on the basis of which dogs relieved themselves during the opening parade. They had sometimes even discussed the quality and quantity of the droppings.

Of course, she remembered Woodlake. She remembered everything. She remembered it too well, in fact, and wished there were a way not to remember so much of the time. She tapped the button on the clock again.

"Five forty-four P.M.," it said. Carmichael seemed peeved with her. Maybe there was something special at Woodlake that he wanted her to remember. Well, if there was, he'd just have to be specific with her. She wasn't going to let her mind just roam willy-nilly all over that time. She'd had enough of that. Poking her fingers into every crevice of the past, smelling this, hefting that, hearing whole conversations replay that were about the most trivial things.

She especially remembered conversations with Cynthia. Cynthia at Woodlake. Oh, that was good. Whenever Cynthia came to Florida for a visit, she'd go along to the dog track sometimes, just to shake her head at the waste of money. Cynthia used to walk back to the betting windows with Carmichael and Arabella and watch them hand over their cash to the men inside their cages. Her eyes clucking.

"You don't like the dogs, do you?" Arabella had asked her once.

"I don't like buying their owners things I can't afford myself."

"What would you have us do with the money instead?"

"It's not mine to do anything with. It's your money. If this is what it takes to make you happy, then I say you are welcome to spend your money this way."

"Thank God for that," Arabella had said.

On those visits Cynthia had always refused to use the condominium trash chute. Each time she brought along her own trash bags from Tennessee and kept them in the guest room till they were full. Then she'd get Carmichael Junior to drive her to some anonymous trash Dumpster in Wood-lake, and she'd throw it away.

Arabella had asked her about it.

"I don't pay to use your trash facilities," Cynthia had said. "I don't want to be beholden."

"What's so special about your trash you don't want it mingling with ours?"

"Oh, no," said Cynthia. "I'm sure the trash coming from a condominium on the ocean like this is way better than any trash me and Carmichael Junior could produce."

Maybe it was better that Arabella had never had children. If one of her own had sassed her like that, she might have done something that would have made her old age truly difficult.

As it was, Arabella just took the gradual decay of her senses and mind as the symmetrical other half of being born. You took nine months to come about and a few years to get up and look around and comment. That there should be the same period of unraveling on the other end was reassuring, comforting in the way that every coherent thing had always comforted Arabella. No, old age and dying were fine. It was just that now with the darkness, there was nothing to do but take stock. Take stock.

"Remember the hospital?" the clock said when she pushed its button later on.

So that was it. So Carmichael wanted her to go over that. It was just like him. There had never been a queasy bone between the two of them. They could either of them fillet a fish or bandage a knife wound or clean up some spillage from their own unfaithful bodies without so much as a held breath or averted eyes.

Arabella had been a daughter of the South, a debutante from New Orleans, where petticoats and lace and wide-brimmed hats and parasols and good strong gentlemen had shielded her from much of what the world called harsh. Still, all the men in her family had been men of the soil, so she'd also known the blood of varmints and livestock, skinned pelts, and even occasionally the smell of human blood.

So when Carmichael could no longer walk to the bathroom, no longer clamp those sphincters, when he could not raise his hand to squeeze the channel selector gun, she had been there. They had talked and she had held his hand and she had hauled him upright and into the bathroom and had stood away as he tried to do at least that for himself.

Cynthia and Carmichael Junior had made a special trip down to Woodlake to attend those final days.

"Have any of his dog track friends come to visit him?" she'd asked Arabella.

"No, why should they?"

"I guess they're too busy gambling."

Carmichael had given her the forgive-and-forget look from his bed. The room had been full of the smell of his dying, and when he sent her that look, nothing pathetic in it, just a quiet, peaceful closing and reopening of his eyes, Arabella almost fainted from the love and sadness and joy she felt for him then.

Maybe that was what he wanted her to remember now, why he had sent his voice through the clock.

She was eating a bowl of Cheerios when Cynthia came later. Her familiar knock sounded at the apartment door, and Arabella called out that the door was unlocked.

Cynthia entered and said nothing more until she was sitting across from Arabella at the cherry dining-room table. It was one of her tricks, but Arabella wasn't frightened by it this time. Arabella could smell the casserole Cynthia had brought. Squash with melted cheese and crushed Saltines for a topping. Arabella loved squash but hated the sharp cheddar Cynthia always used.

"You decided not to wait for the squash," Cynthia said. "Wanted Cheerios instead."

"I like Cheerios."

"It's five-thirty in the afternoon," Cynthia said.

"I know the time. That's the one thing I know."

Cynthia stood and brought the gold cube clock over to the dining-room table.

His voice said aloud, "Four-fifteen A.M."

Arabella ate another spoonful of the Cheerios.

"I'll put the squash in the refrigerator then. You won't forget it, will you?"

"Why would I do that?"

"Do you want me to reset your clock?"

"It's fine how it is."

"Why don't I take it with me to the jewelry story tomorrow and see if they can fix it?"

"No," Arabella said. She held out her hand for the clock, but Cynthia held on to it.

"Yes. It's useless like it is. It just throws you off."

"I like it like it is. It doesn't matter if I go with the rest of the world anyway. Give it to me." She kept her hand out there.

"You spilled Cheerios all over the Congoleum."

"I want that clock. Put it in my hand."

"All right, all right."

Arabella set the clock beside her cereal bowl and felt around the tablecloth for her spoon. She was sure Cynthia had moved it. After a while she discovered it resting in the bowl.

"Cynthia," she said, "I want you to do something for me."

"Yes."

"I want you to tell me what you remember from that time at Woodlake, the last time." As she was saying it, she felt herself losing her balance, falling, sailing down ten flights inside herself. Why in goodness' name was she inviting Cynthia to talk about this?

But Cynthia didn't let a heartbeat pass and said, "I remember eating supper at Benny Dee's Restaurant, having to send the pork chop back."

"I mean something important," Arabella said. "Something that might have been important but that we didn't pay any attention to at the time."

"Arabella, you shouldn't dwell on that time now, dear. It's morbid."

Arabella touched her hair, let a finger rest on the edge of the talking clock.

"Something we said or did, something that happened that might have been of importance."

"Well, I don't like to say it," Cynthia said, walking into the kitchen with that aromatic casserole. "But I believe you were very badly overcharged on that casket. I checked into it when we got back, and you could have had the exact same box for seven hundred and fifty dollars less from Fuqua's."

Arabella remembered it now. It was surely why Carmichael had spoken through the clock, prompting her to recall Woodlake. It had been one of those exhausted conversations in the car on the way to a restaurant, taking a short recess from the hospital. Cynthia had been talking about one of her boys, how much he ate, five hard-boiled eggs every morning so he could make the wrestling team. And Arabella had said five hard-boiled eggs could get in there and clog your arteries. And Cynthia had let a few seconds pass and then said, "Arabella, how'd you get to know so much about mothering?"

Carmichael Junior had said something then, swinging them away from this moment back to the trivial.

Arabella rested the spoon in her Cheerios bowl and said, "Can you forgive me?"

Cynthia let the refrigerator door whoosh shut. She'd had it open for a few minutes, probably making a pathetic tally of all the spoilage there.

"What in the world are you yakking about now?"

"I'm old," Arabella said. "I'm almost out of here."

"No, you're not, honey. You got as much kick in you as ever. But you should eat this squash casserole instead of Cheerios. Now, that's for sure."

"I have not given you love," she said. "I have never been able to show love for you."

"Don't be silly," Cynthia said. "I love you. You love me. Everything's fine between us."

"No," Arabella said. "I've never loved you. I should have, I wanted to. I want to now."

"You are the silliest thing in the world."

"Let me have your hand," Arabella said. "Let me be your mother. Just for a few minutes. Nobody needs to know."

"You really ought to try that squash casserole. I made it just like you like it with extra-sharp cheddar. It's still warm." Cynthia went across to the refrigerator again and retrieved the casserole. She clinked around in the cabinet till she got a dish she wanted and then found a serving spoon. She dished out some of the casserole, brought it over, and placed it before Arabella. Arabella sat and smelled it.

"You should try it. It's good manners."

Arabella took a taste. She kept seeing that forgive-and-forget look on Carmichael's face and tried to put it on her own. She swallowed the bite of casserole and told Cynthia it was even better than usual.

Cynthia stayed until she'd finished the whole plate. At the door she said, "You know, if you'd just get over your snobbery about television, it'd let you know what time of day it is. And it can be very beneficial to get involved in other people's troubles. It makes your own worries seem so measly."

When she'd left, Arabella felt for the clock. It wasn't beside her plate. She rose and made a complete tour of the apartment. She patted down every inch of the dining-room table. It wasn't in the kitchen. Or the living room.

Arabella sat on the couch, her hands resting in her lap. Underwood's Jewelry would fix the clock, get it set right. But she was sure they'd kill Carmichael's voice, tampering with it. That was the end of it then. She sat for a while feeling the light pass through her, feeling the stuffy air of her apartment flood in and out of her body.

"Remember the hospital?" Carmichael had been in the hospital for only two weeks before the coma drew him down into it. There were only those two weeks to recall. But when you thought about it hard, really pictured it, two weeks had a lot of nooks, a lot of words and glances. There were months of time buried in those two weeks, all those touches they had traded, the mild heat his dying had given off. Those two weeks could keep her busy for a long while, if she could bear it.

PAPER
PRODUCTS

I

$\mathcal{R}$ussell Prunty developed an interest in plumbing at the age of ten. That was the year his father ran off with a Negro and his mother burned down her first house. Russell had snuck back to the burned-out remains almost every day for a month and had marveled at the pipes still holding up the bathroom sink, the blackened shower pipe, which looked to him like a rattler reared up to strike, and the toilet bowl full of soot and ash but still rooted to the foundation.

His mother burned down three more houses before it became clear to everyone in Hazleton, Tennessee, that she was a risk as a renter. Russell and his two sisters and mother were living with Russell's aunt Brenda when the sheriff came by to tell Mrs. Prunty that enough was enough. Having three kids and a husband who ran off with a Negro was about equal to four burned-down houses. But if there was so much as even a backyard barbecue from here on out, he'd move her pronto into an asbestos cell.

Russell was fifteen when he went to work for Al Pink's Plumbing Company. Al owned three VW vans that he'd painted pink, and by the time Russell had turned sixteen, he was driving one of them full time. There wasn't a plumber that'd ever worked for Al who had Russell's love for the job. Russell Prunty would scooch under foundations every hour of the day or night; he'd bend double under sinks, ram his arm up to the elbow into somebody else's hair clogs and sludge, and come up beaming. Ask him to muck around in a septic tank, drain a cesspool, wade into a bathroom to snake out a toilet, why, he'd do it without a flinch. And good golly, Miss Molly, did he love to drive that pink van.

When Russell was seventeen, Al took him one Sunday afternoon to Tobacco Road Racecourse in nearby Murphytown. They watched the Chevies and Fords stir up the dust all afternoon, Russell unsure of why he was there. He caught Al sneaking looks at him off and on. As they were leaving, sunburned and nearly deaf, Al asked Russell if he'd ever hankered to drive like that on a Sunday afternoon. Around and round like that, flat-out.

"Yeah, that wouldn't be too bad," Russell said.

" 'Cause I got an idea." Al opened the driver door and waved Russell in to drive the pink Olds. "You see all those people?"

"I saw 'em. There was a bunch of 'em."

"They're staring at those cars, for what, three, four hours? Near to hypnotized as they could get."

"Yes, sir, that's a fact." Russell had a whiff of what was coming.

"Now what if one of those cars wasn't a car at all, but a

van? A pink one and it had AL PINK'S PLUMBING, WE'LL CLEAN YOU OUT WITHOUT CLEANING YOU OUT, on the side of it? How many times you think all those people would see it in one afternoon?"

"I never raced on any oval track. Nowhere for that matter."

"Fifty times, a hundred? You know how much that would cost me in radio time?"

"I do race around town now and then."

"You wouldn't be expected to win, boy. The point is, just get around and around and let them read the sign."

Russell Prunty raced the pink van every weekend for over a year. Little by little he'd bored out the VW engine, channeled the body so it settled lower over the frame, added wider tires, and even moved the engine up to midway to keep the center of gravity lower. He'd never placed better than second, but still, it was the first VW van anybody had ever seen on a stock track, and people paid attention.

The year Russell turned nineteen, Al made him a present of the van.

"You earned it, Prunty," he said. "Pink's a household name now."

Russell moved all his jeans and T-shirts and his radio and tools into the van and started sleeping in it. To his surprise, he began to enjoy sleeping. Though his mother hadn't so much as lit a birthday candle in five years, Russell had never slept all that well down the hall from her.

He also lost his X-ray vision dream. He'd been dreaming it for so long that he assumed it was his dream, the one dream he'd been given to dream. While walking down a street in a town he'd never seen, Russell had the power to see through the walls of every house and building. He saw through to the plumbing, through bricks and drywall and wood, to the house's skeleton of copper tubing, lead drainage pipes, steel indoor piping. All of it sprouting from the ground like a daffy metal tree. With the house blooming around it like leaves.

Russell informed Al that he was quitting.

"What took you so long?"

"Whew," Russell said, "I thought you'd do 'after-all-I-done-for-you.' "

"After all I done for you, I think you got better things in store. You should go flat-out after them."

"I thought I'd drive down to Georgia, Alabama and try my luck at some of the tracks down there."

"I expect to be reading about you someday, boy. But listen here, somebody's flushing their john this second in Hazleton and it's gurgling back at them. If you need to come home, there'll always be some backed-up shit waiting for you."

"Much appreciated," Russell said.

He told his mother, and she asked if there was a Negro involved in it anywhere.

"No, Mama," he told her. "And I don't want to hear you been playing with matches again, either."

"My burning days are long gone, boy. Look at me. Do I look like I could ever light anything up again?"

Before he left, he painted out AL PINK'S PLUMBING and the slogan, and he stenciled in his name. Then he stepped back to look at it and think. He added an apostrophe and an *s,* and then he stopped again. Russell Prunty's what? He thought for a few minutes, decided it was right like it was, and drove on out of Hazleton as soon as the paint was dry.

For nine years he worked his way down Georgia, across

Alabama, into Louisiana, then Texas. There was a war on, but no one official or otherwise knew where he was. There had been one woman who believed he should marry her, but he didn't have that ambition. When he pictured his life a year or two ahead, he pictured what he'd just done that day, going all-out around a flat dirt track or scrabbling around in somebody's attic to patch a hot-water leak.

Into the eighth of those nine years he picked up a dog in Port Arthur. It had tagged around him in the pits at Memorial Speedway for a few days, and when all the other drivers had left, the dog was curled up in front of Russell's van. Russell let him come aboard.

"It's turning into a long trip I'm taking," Russell told the dog. "It's OK for Russell Prunty, but some folks couldn't stand the pace."

The dog thumped its gold, mangy tail on cue.

"Well," he said, "what'll I call you?"

He called the dog Russell Prunty's Dog. He knew it was an eccentric name, but that was OK Russell had gotten a reputation as an eccentric. One or two of the speedway announcers had used the word about the pink van, still lettered RUSSELL PRUNTY'S, and he figured it also applied to him, now that his hair had gotten to his shoulders and he had this beard that looked like the moths had gotten to.

Truth was, he liked the word *eccentric.* It'd gotten him out of a bar fight in Tuscaloosa. Some cowboy tobacco farmer had crowed to his friends that there was a shit-fer-brains hippie among them. Before the cowboy could get his friends stirred up, Russell went over to their table and told the cowboy he wasn't any goddamn draft-dodging son of a bitch hippie, he was a sorry-assed-stock-car-racing eccentric, so leave his ass alone.

For nine years he kept rolling. Most of what he learned

he learned from the radio talk shows and late-night sermons and newscasts. He didn't know how to be lonely. Since he'd never had but Al Pink as a friend, he scarcely knew what friends were or why the people calling in on the late-night talk shows made such a fuss over having or not having one.

He'd slept with only a handful of women, and they were the ones who slumped against him in midnight bars or who pranced down into the pits after a race and started peeling out of their clothes as they climbed into the pink van. And even with them he never dared sleep afterward, his ears hair-triggered for the scrape of a match.

He drove south through Texas until there were no more ovals, and finally until there was no more plumbing. He was twenty-eight and out of the territory where what he knew could buy groceries.

At the border crossing in Laredo, Russell Prunty's Dog got down from the van and wandered back toward America. Russell drove on into Mexico, a little amazed at what he was doing, but reminding himself that he was an adventurer now and an eccentric and that it was turning out to be his purpose in life to do the oddball thing.

Two days, three, he wound up the tight rough roads into the Sierra Madre Orientals. Even though the calluses on his hands, he could feel the burn from gripping the wheel through switchback after switchback. He made it up to a dreary, startled village named China before he threw a rod and had to stop.

II

In the middle of July a little more than a year later, he was still waiting for the rod to be delivered from Mexico City.

He'd taken to panning for gold in the cold streams that ran out of the Sierras, and he was sharing a one-room adobe hut with an Indian he'd named Al Pink. Their cabin had a dirt floor, a cot made from pine with a mattress stuffed with pine needles, and one open window that looked down on the village of China.

One Mexican in the village who had a little English had told Russell that there wasn't any gold in this part of Mexico.

"You ever looked?" Prunty had asked him.

The Mexican told him there was no need to look. All you needed to do was try to dig a hole in the ground and you would find there was nothing but slate. Slate with two inches of dust over it.

"That'll make it that much better then, when I find it." Everything that Russell knew about gold mining had come from one movie he'd seen in some motel in Louisiana late at night. It appealed to him, though. Not so much the idea of being rich, but more the idea that you could find gold lying right there among the dust and slate. In the movie he had seen, the prospector had finally found a load of the stuff, right at the end of the movie, and he didn't even bother going down into town to cash in. That really impressed Russell.

The Mexican from the village told him that his friend Al Pink was loco.

"What makes you think I ain't loco?"

"North American loco," said the Mexican, "isn't the real thing. Mexican loco, this is true loco."

But Russell and Al got along fine, and the days were simple and quiet without any sign of gold. The little savings he'd accumulated from his winnings were enough of a grubstake to last him maybe a year.

It was about suppertime early in July when Russell heard a motor straining up his hill. Al Pink ran into the adobe cabin to hide, but Russell stood up from panning, brushed himself off, and waited for the invaders to arrive.

There were three of them in a VW van, a lot like Russell's only it was painted with peace signs and crude drawings of unicorns. Down from the van stepped a short, plumpish girl with straight black hair. She dragged a duffel bag out of the rear of the van and slammed the door shut. The van U-turned and went bumping back down the path. Russell Prunty walked over to her. She was prettier up close. It was her eyes, gray and hooded, and her nose, not exactly a beak, but larger than normal, which seemed sexy to Russell.

"You the American?" she asked him.

"I'm from Tennessee," he said. "Hazleton. Near Three Heads."

She searched the clouds for something.

"I'm Macu Smith from Florida."

Russell said he was pleased to meet her and shook her small hand.

"I was traveling across country to San Francisco with these two guys, but they just turned gay in New Orleans and I couldn't hack it any longer. Not that I object to it, but it's just yucky to listen to, you know?"

He didn't, but he shook his head knowingly.

"What kind of name is that, Mackyou?"

"Macu. Short for Inmaculada. It's like, ironic now."

"That's the first one of those I've come across."

"My mother's Cuban. My father's the Smith."

"My mother used to burn down houses."

"That's nice," she said, eyeing his hut. "You live in that?"

"Yeah, it's mud. Better than asbestos for fireproof."

She raved and raved about the view. She kept gazing around. Russell had never paid much attention to the place. But she kept staring out at the mountain ranges and saying, "Far-out, far far-out." Russell stared with her at those dirty, grubby hills while she raved and raved.

While he was showing her the inside of the adobe hut, she pulled out some Kleenex from her jacket and blew her nose. Russell thought that she must be weepy, that it was hitting her all of a sudden that here she was stranded in the hills of another country.

"You got any Kleenex around this place?" she asked him.

He sent Al Pink down the mountain to get some Kleenex, and then he showed Macu the stream where he was panning. She didn't say much, ask any questions, or even seem much impressed with Russell's search for gold.

By the next morning she'd ripped through the two boxes of tissues and Al Pink had to go back down the mountain for more.

"You have a cold," said Russell as he stooped over the stream with his pan.

"No," she said. "I just got a lot of snot in me."

"That's eccentric," he said.

"If you need to give it a name, then that's your problem."

"I *like* eccentric."

"I'm a psychology major," Macu told him. "I guess I'm in a little better position to say what's normal and what isn't."

"You sure go through paper products, is all I'm saying."

Al Pink left after a week. All the trudging up and back and the sleeping outside the adobe hut while she was in there honking and snorting all night. By the end of August she was pregnant.

It was the adobe moonlight and the barn owl that started hooting from a cypress tree. It was her with her know-it-all voice, her large reddened nose, her raving about the view. It was different from the other times he'd been to bed with women. She wasn't lovey-dovey with him, didn't even seem to like to kiss, but she sure could thrash around. There he was, all of a sudden in love. No longer smelling for the sulfur flare of a match, no longer hugging a monkey wrench in the night, and for once thinking that maybe it wouldn't be so bad to pull into the pits, shut off the motor, tune it down to street legal, and be a daddy.

"I never wanted to be some gold miner's wife," she told him one morning, after a night of staring out the cabin window and him staring at the back of her head.

"I can do plenty of other things."

"I'm a psychology major, not some eccentric gold miner's appendage. You're going to have to take me up to Del Rio or Laredo or wherever so I can get on a Greyhound. I'll get my daddy to wire me some money, or something."

"You said how you hated your daddy."

"I'm going back and finish being a psychology major."

"How about him?" Russell pointed to her belly.

"She'll be a psychology major, too."

"I'll be one too then, goddamn it."

She snorted at Russell. Then started in on the Kleenex.

He repaired the engine, making a production of it so Macu might be impressed. When he finally fired it up, something lit again inside him. Florida, he thought, more adventure. What an oddball thing, going to Florida to be somebody's husband.

Macu and Russell arrived in Orlando two days before her college started. Russell let her out at her daddy's house and she skipped on inside and there he was, without an idea of what he was supposed to do. So he put on the emergency brake, sucked on a warm beer, and watched a girl mailman making the rounds through that spanking fresh neighborhood.

It was a subdivision called Wynken, Blynken and Nod Estates. Her daddy's house was on Thumper Thoroughfare. He was one of the contractors slapping the place up, getting ready for more Disney World growth. Not a lot of grass yet, fresh asphalt streets, houses all alike except for the shutters being different colors, and short streetlights, the kind you could reach up and change a bulb in.

Macu hadn't said diddly to him across two thousand miles. Everything told him he should turn the van around and head on back to his stream in Mexico. He was fiddling with the ignition key, a half twist away from hightailing it, when there was her daddy in his window.

"You the perpetrator?"

Russell just stared at the man, trying to recall where he was.

"You the father, boy?"

"It isn't born yet," he said. "I mean, I will be, I'm ready to be and all that, if she's going to have it."

"Watch what you say to me," he said. "We don't have the word *abortion* in our vocabulary."

Russell told him that yes, yes, sir, he was indeed the father. He wanted badly to get out of the van, but the man was pressing his belly against the door. He wore a starched white shirt with the name Hartford Smith stitched over the pocket.

"You take drugs, I suppose."

"I smoke a cigarette now and again."

"You won't do that around me. Not even on my lawn. Or in the street outside my house."

"All righty."

"You consider yourself a hippie."

"I been gold mining up where the barbers ain't made it yet."

"You'll cut it neat and clean, or I'll cut it myself. And how old are you?"

He told him.

"She's just turned nineteen," he said.

"She acts older."

"You enjoyed yourself pretty good, didn't you?"

Russell couldn't answer that one.

"Which part you like best? You like to lick her, don't you? I can see you're the licking sort."

"If you stand back a bit, I'll get down out of here and shake your hand and try to convince you I'm not some bum."

"She's in there right now telling her mother what a slut she's become. And that little girl is the only speck of joy in her mama's life. You think I want to shake your hand? The goddamn hand that groped my own flesh and blood?" Hartford hawked up a dollop of spit and sent it across the street. He wiped his mouth with a Kleenex he had in his shirt pocket.

"What kind of honest work you know how to do?"

"I'm a plumber and a car racer and a mechanic."

"It figures," he said, and stalked back inside his house.

Russell sat in his van watching that mailgirl passing out bills all up and down that new street. It was the first mailgirl he'd ever seen.

"Something else has started happening since you been gone, Russell Prunty. Whooee, hang on. We're going round and round."

Late in September Macu and Russell were living five blocks away in one of those houses. It'd taken three days for the carpenters to unload the forms from a railroad car, cart them over to the sandy lot, nail them all together, and hand him the key. Nothing down, 375 a month, another 150 a month for rental furniture, and there you go.

Russell had watched them as they glued the white plastic PVC plumbing together. Not a piece of copper or lead or steel in the whole place. You set a house like that on fire, it would melt the plumbing in a second. It was enough to give Russell his X-ray dream back again.

He was spending his days in retired people's toilets. There was always something wrong with a retiree's toilet. Usually it was because they tried to flush a flower pot or something down the drain. He'd be in there snaking out the john and up would come some old geranium stalks and they'd say, "Goodness gracious, where in the world did that come from?"

"From your toilet," Russell would tell them.

He figured that old people were just too tired to take their garbage out to the street. They'd just flush it away. This and that. Old photographs and engagement rings. Stockings with tears in them and savings bonds. Forget panning for gold, Russell would say, you want to get rich, put on some rubber pants and go wading through the sewers of Orlando, Florida.

Macu spent her days at the university, and at night she'd pile her books up all around her desk and set a box of Kleenex off to one side and spend the night flipping through pages and filling up the wicker wastebasket by her desk.

It embarrassed Russell to take out the garbage on Mondays and Thursdays. There would be all his neighbors with their two black bags or twin cans, and there he'd be smiling at them like nothing was wrong, stacking six, seven oversize bags on his sidewalk. All of them chocked full of Kleenex and paper towels. There was nothing that got damp in their house that didn't require about half a roll of towels to sop it up. "Why not use a sponge and save them towels?" Russell might say. And she'd shoot back something like "It's OK for you, you're used to living in muck and mire, but I come from a family that's clean."

Russell had no way of knowing about that since he'd still never been invited inside the Smith house. Never even met Macu's mother.

"I'm trying to spare her the grief of having to see what I did to myself," Macu told him.

"I'm that bad, why're you living with me?"

"Why do you think, Mr. Psychology?"

"I'm not as dumb as you make me out. I understand a few things. I spend a good bit of my time pondering."

"You don't know beans, Russell Prunty. You don't know why the sky's blue. You didn't even know how to say 'menstruation' till you met me."

"You stay with me," he said. "But you treat me like a dog."

"Bowwow, Russell. Bowwow, bowwow."

"Why is that?"

She blew her nose and punched her glasses back into

place. It was Friday night. Russell had been wanting to take the van out to a local speedway that night and stretch it out a bit. But Macu assembled her books around her as usual and had set about reading and sniffling.

"I think you're trying to upset your daddy, is why. I think you hate him 'cause of how he never lets your mother leave the house. You knew he'd have a fit over me, and that's why you picked out someplace to live so nearby. And I think you study all those books 'cause you want to figure out why you're so unhappy."

She was staring at him then.

"And I think I know why you blow your nose all the time."

"Russell . . ." she warned him.

"You got stuff inside you you want to get out, but you don't know how. I know that, 'cause I got stuff inside me, too."

"Shit is what you got inside you."

Russell got up out of one of these rented armchairs and walked over to the phony fireplace.

"I been asking myself why I stay around and put up with it," he said. "I guess it's the adventure of it. It's the adventure."

"You are some kind of fool, you know that? Living with somebody isn't any adventure."

"It is so far."

Macu took off her glasses and laid them on the desk. She drew open the middle drawer of her desk and started fumbling around in there for something. Russell felt relieved. He sat back down and let out some breath. He'd been thinking and figuring what it was that was wrong between them, and now he'd spoken it, gotten all that balled-up mess out.

Macu found what she was looking for and swiveled her desk chair around and bent over to the bottom of the drapes. Russell couldn't see what she was doing down there, but then he heard the flinty scratch of a lighter and saw Macu's face flare up.

She was sprawled on the terrazzo floor. Russell had opened all the windows and drapes to air out that smoke smell. He was panting a little still.

"You tried to kill us both, and her, too."

"I don't want her. I don't want any of it."

"You don't have to want me, but you got to want her. Mothers feel that way, no matter what."

"Mr. Seen-the-world-and-knows-all-the-mysteries-of-life."

"I seen some things. But I haven't seen any mothers didn't get their children up and out of a burning house."

"If you think I'm going to let this girl get born and have you pawing her, then you don't have sense God gave a green apple."

"Do what?"

"You heard me. And don't think I don't know what you and my daddy talk about. He tells my mother and she tells me."

"I said exactly eight words to your daddy since we been in Florida. What is it I'm supposed to be talking to him about?"

"Me," she said. "Sex. All that. You think I don't know men? I know men. I never met one didn't want to play doctor with a six-year-old. You picked me 'cause I was so much younger. I was about as young as you could get away with, without it being illegal."

"Oh, man." Russell managed to grin and shake his head.

"I see now why your two boyfriends turned queer."

"Men seduce your mothers and then they start in on the daughters."

Russell jerked to his feet.

"Your daddy. Did that? Did he, Macu? I'll walk over there and beat him till his face runs down his shirt."

"No," she said, and stood up, too. "We need a nap."

"What?"

"A nap, Russell. Remember naps?"

"You couldn't be in any mood for that."

"Don't tell me how I feel, please. You want to or not?"

"Well. I heard about pregnant women being fickle, but, boy."

Macu led the way down the hall, untying her sweat pants on the way, walking out of them, wriggling out of her sweat shirt. By the bedroom door she was down to her white socklets.

Russell followed, dazed and still a bit groggy from the fumes the drapes had given off.

"I made a mess."

Russell heard her, but he was too asleep to answer.

"I made a mess in the bathroom," she said.

He rolled over. She was sitting up beside him, her back against the wood grain headboard.

"You sound sick."

"I'm a little weak, is all."

"She OK?"

"I was on the john, blowing my nose, and she just let go. It wasn't my fault." There was no smart-ass in her voice at all.

Russell stepped out of bed and into three inches of water.

He waded into the bathroom and shut off the water in the toilet. He couldn't see anything in the dark, but he could smell something that in all his days in backed-up messes he had never smelled.

He waded back into the bedroom and put on his pants.

"You need a doctor or anything?"

"I'm sorry, Russell. I am. I truly am."

He handed her a box of Kleenex that was sitting on the bureau.

"I'm going out to the van for some tools. But I can call for a doctor first, if you think that's what you need."

"Go ahead, clean up the mess. I'm all right."

He sloshed through the living room and on outside. The moon was ripe and shining directly, it seemed, onto his van.

RUSSELL PRUNTY'S, it still read.

Russell Prunty's what?

Russell Prunty's going to snake out his own kid. Or, Russell Prunty's going to take out his keys, start up his van, and drive back to where the plumbing is made from metal.

Or, Russell Prunty's latest adventure turns ugly.

How about, Russell Prunty's home?

No, this is it, Russell Prunty's near to home as he's ever going to get.

He took out both the snake and the plunger. Suck it out or force it on through the crimp, whichever way worked.

POETIC
DEVICES

My language is a great two-headed fish that lives only in one pond in a remote mountain region. No other two-headed fish exists, and the greatest experts say that my two-headed language has no relatives in the whole world. This fish is Basque.

But it didn't take me long to understand that if I wanted to be the richest man I could be, I would have to leave behind my language. I would have to learn to speak in American.

I moved to Vermont.

This is in the country of America, where everybody owns something expensive. Usually they own a very fast car. This is necessary because in America it is said, "Time is money."

I came to Vermont, America, because I wished to become rich. It was an impractical wish. For everyone in that country wants the same thing. Two hundred and forty-four million wishes, and all exactly the same. The air is packed with this wish.

But I believed my wish would happen, for I was using an approach that appeared most unusual. I wanted to become rich by writing poems in this language.

I had learned that there was only one rich poet in America. He lived in California. This is the reason I chose Vermont. In a country so big, I was certain that there was room for at least two rich poets. This appeared reasonable.

The other reason I lived in Vermont was that it was the home of Robert Frost who said, "Free verse is like playing tennis with the net down." I believe Mr. Robert Frost became a rich man because of ideas like this. All verse should cost something, like a tennis ball.

This is also the part of America where another rich poet once lived. The most famous and wise and rich Mr. R. Waldo Emerson. He said, "I think nothing is of any value in books, excepting the transcendental and extraordinary." I agree with this sentence, too.

One more sentence I agree with is: "The death of a beautiful woman is unquestionably the most poetical topic in the world—and it is beyond doubt that the lips best suited for such a topic are those of a bereaved lover." This was said by a man named Allan Poe who never became very rich, but it was only because he died in a gutter before people got to know how great he was. If Mr. Allan Poe had not died in this gutter, he would be a rich poet today.

I found a beautiful woman who was also extraordinary. And she was also a user of the form of meditation named transcendental. This is a word very hard for me to pronounce. Her name was Fay Trigger. This sounded like a beautiful name to me, and I used it in several of my poems.

Fay Trigger worked in a bar in the town I picked to grow rich in. The bar's name was Snowdrop. This is poetical, too. Here is Fay, and how she talked:

"One more night in this jerkwater hole and I'll puke. If I didn't have such a damn good disposition, I'd cut the throat of the next bastard that walked in here drunk looking for a warm fanny to pinch."

Some of her words were so extraordinary they were not in my dictionary.

She was beautiful, too. Her hair was blond, and sometimes when she woke in the morning and I turned on the fluorescent light above the bed, I could see a rainbow of green and blue shining through her hair.

I bought her many things to show her my love for her.

Much of the money Grandmother gave me I spent on the beautiful jewelry and perfumes she was used to wearing. She also liked beer and chocolate.

I was happy. For when I came to Vermont, I knew nobody and could speak only a few lines from poems I had memorized and some other words that would buy food for me. And then all at once I had a lover, with blond hair. The next morning after Fay Trigger and I fell into our love, I wrote my first poem in America.

Everywhere I read it I was successful; money was thrown to me. It seemed to be a wonderful country for poets. People who wanted to be rich themselves still knew when they saw a man with a good idea, and they helped him become rich by this extraordinary custom of money throwing.

Sometimes the poor ones threw pieces of their food. I

knew for sure that I was not playing with my net down.

Fay Trigger wanted to blow this hole. By this she meant she wanted us to travel so I could grow richer by reading my poems in bars across the country of America.

Without once forgetting the wise words I had memorized in my bedroom in the Basque country, I set off with Fay Trigger. When we sat down on the bus, and it began to move, Fay Trigger said this:

"I got more baggage than I bargained for on this one. It's like being responsible for a retarded gerbil."

This is a simile. It is a very poetic device. Fay Trigger, whose blond hair was now red for our travels, had learned this simile idea from my poems.

We stopped in the largest city in America and bought a hot breakfast where the buses arrived. I looked into a newspaper while Fay Trigger talked to an American policeman. She was a friendly woman. She said this:

"Creeps and worms. I'm too softhearted and the creeps and worms see it right off and then, what do you know, I'm a mother hen all of a sudden."

Very poetic. I couldn't help myself. I listened while I pretended to look at the heaviest newspaper ever made. This is an hyperbole. It is one of my best devices. I use it to put humor in a poem. If I think someone is beautiful, like Fay Trigger, I will say, "Her voice outsung the choir." This means it is easy to hear Fay Trigger even if there are a hundred people talking at once, like at the bus station.

In my newspaper I saw an advertisement for a poetry reading. The richest poet in America was to read his poems that night! He had come on a bus all the way from California to do this to me. This news made me lose my hunger. I had hoped that this poet from California would be content to stay home. But I then knew that like me, he must have been given so much money from his neighbors that he had to go away. Heavy fish swam in my stomach.

The policeman who had listened to Fay Trigger asked me a question. I did not hear him at first. Then I heard him.

"You deaf?" he asked me.

I felt very sad about this rich poet coming to New York City. Now I would have to go to another town, because he would take all the money for poetry from this town. Then I thought, No, I will stay here, and not run away like a nanny goat. I will let them choose between my poetry and the richest poet in America's.

Again the policeman asked me something.

"Let's see some ID."

I said, "No, I can't see any right now. I must write a new poem about this sadness."

"I want to see some identification," he said to me. He sounded unhappy, too.

"You'll have to see it alone, sir," is what I answered. He seemed to be a very lonely man. He needed a friend like Fay Trigger. Fay Trigger? Fay Trigger! She had gone.

I stood up and picked up my satchel full of socks and poems. This is a zeugma. It is rare and difficult. It is only the second zeugma I have ever written. My first one was: "Fay Trigger threw her shadow and empty beer can out the front door."

Fay Trigger had vanished. There were people everywhere in that big room hurrying, slouching, spying, sleeping, but none of them was Fay Trigger. The big fish swimming in my belly took a deep dive.

The lonely policeman said to me this:

"The lady had a bus to catch."

This sounded like a poetry device to me. It reminded me of what is called a euphemism.

"A bus to catch," is all I could say. But I knew this meant not a bus, but it meant Fay Trigger had died out of my life. The fish in my bowels swam quickly up into my heart and then my neck. Allan Poe, the poor poet, had experienced something similar.

The policeman used these words on me next:

"OK there, creep, let's move on."

With my satchel by my side I walked with this policeman out into the dreary, clouded day. This device is called objective correlative. It means the sun felt just the way I did.

"The square garden is in what place?" I asked this policeman.

He pointed with his big stick.

Oh, the feelings that poured through me as I walked toward the famous square garden. The feelings were too many to feel at once. The big fish was now many minnows. This is called alliteration. It is easy to do. I sometimes have done it without even meaning to. Each minnow was feeding on the new buds of my heart. These new buds had grown just to hold the love I had felt for Fay Trigger.

I sat down on the sidewalk before a store selling books for adults and wrote a poem. It came to me so fast that I had not any time to use paper. I wrote it on my hand. It was for Fay Trigger, and it was the greatest poem in the Western world. This is another hyperbole.

When I had finished, I had to hurry to reach the square garden in time for the richest poet in America. I stood in a line of people. It was a cold night, and many of these people were wearing fur coats. And for pants, blue jeans. This seemed paradoxical to me.

I made small changes in the poem on my hand. I crossed out many adjectives. I put in some synesthesia. This is a device that I like. If you felt great sadness for, let us say, losing Fay Trigger, you might say, "The cold empty odor of mink fur filled the dusk." This is too complicated for me to explain. But I understand it anyway.

When I gave my money to the man in the window, he gave me a ticket. I counted the money of my grandmother. It took me only a few seconds to do this. When I first came to America, it would take me almost five minutes to count my money. This is progress.

There were thousands of people inside the square garden. All of them whispering like a congregation before Holy Communion. I sat behind two young women who had long blond hair. Their hair fell over the backs of their seats and lay on my leg. This picture made me remember Fay Trigger and the night I met her, and how her blond hair lay open like a dancer's fan down the back of her blue coat. I wanted to touch the hair that lay on my knee, but the small fish bubbling in my heart kept me from moving.

Fay Trigger had said this when I told her about my love for her sunlight hair:

"I never met a black-haired man yet didn't want to jump on a blonde. And next week, if I want me a blond boy-friend, I just get out the black dye bottle."

Fay Trigger. I read the poem on my hand quietly to my-self. The fat girl in a raincoat beside me looked at me and said, "You sure you got the right seat?" She made me re-member Fay Trigger. Fish tickled my throat. They swam behind my eyes, fluttering as they went.

Just then all the lights blacked out and the curtains rolled open and there, in a spot of light, stood the richest poet in America. He stood behind a table much like the table where Fay Trigger and I ate our bean sandwiches. He wore blue jeans and a coat and a shirt for sweating and a tie around his neck. His beard was gray. Behind him there was a white refrigerator. And in his hand was a bad headache. This is a device I don't use much because it is too hard to pronounce. It is called metonymy. I meant to say that in his hands was a very large jug of wine.

This confused me until I remembered what the rich R. Waldo Emerson said: "Bards love wine, mead, narcotics, coffee, tea, opium, the fumes of sandalwood and tobacco or whatever species of animal exhilaration." R. Waldo Emerson would have loved Fay Trigger. They also would have agreed on things because she was transcendental. This means she enjoyed sitting in a chair with her eyes closed and trying to stay awake.

The richest poet in America took a long drink from his bottle, and everyone applauded except me. The blond hair on my knee flipped up and down. And the fat girl in the raincoat was the last person to stop her clapping. She wore a wide grin. I asked her what this meant, this wine drinking.

"It means he's drunk out of his gourd," is what she said to me, without looking away from the richest poet.

Then the poet walked over to the refrigerator and opened the door of it. The refrigerator was full of beer cans. It was not clear to me if he preferred wine or this beer.

Once again the audience around me clapped. The fat girl in the raincoat stomped her feet repeatedly and continued to clap after everyone had stopped.

The poet took out a beer can and ripped the opener off like he was tearing the head off a bluebird. This is another simile. For the third time the audience applauded. There were those who whistled. The fat girl was among them.

No poems had been read yet, but still the audience had

clapped very hard, and if they had not given already their money to the man outside, they would have no doubt thrown their money to the stage.

Then he began to talk, and what he said was not poetry. Here is some of it:

"This beats the living crud out of working for a living. It used to be I'd lie around in a damn pus-infested hotel and pull the shades down and get plastered and feel sorry for myself. Gawd, now I stay in the Hilton, have a boy bring me some Jamaican rum, and get plastered and count my money. I mean, I don't understand this almighty country."

Once more there was cheering and applause. The richest poet in America was having trouble standing up. He had one hand on the table where his wine bottle was, and this hand was continuing to slip. The wine bottle on the table fell onto its side and rolled off the table. It smashed on the stage floor.

The clapping for this was very loud. People began to talk to each other. The fat girl in the raincoat said, "Shhhhhh."

He said more then:

"I mean nobody gives three hoots in hell about poetry. I don't think they ever did. I remember when I was in school, before they discovered I was a damn pervert and had my ass removed, there was a teacher went on and on about this poem and that poem. Saying it was beautiful 'cause it was full of this message or that message. I mean, if you want messages, hang around the telegraph office, is what I say."

The fat girl loved this remark, and to prove it, she whistled and stomped her feet at once. The two blond girls in front of me decided there were other things they had to do, and they left.

The richest poet in America threw his beer can at the audience and went to the refrigerator for another one. He came back and sat on the edge of his table and said this:

"I mean, I don't have diddly squat to say to the world. What can I tell a Hindu or a Muslim or a Republican?" Many people laughed now. I felt sad for the richest poet in America. He was trying very hard to remember a poem so he could begin. But he had been given some bad wine. This is what he said next:

"I'm just a wino and a stupid jerk from Pasadena who sleeps under the freeway and has whores for sweethearts. What can I tell old Miss Crampedy Britches about anything? I ain't in the hills and dales and china teacup business." At this moment the richest poet in America fell off the table. He lay kicking his legs like a beetle on his back. He tried to stand up, but the great strong hand of wine pressed him down. This is personification.

The fat girl beside me laughed hard at this; then she stood up in her seat and looked very serious. Two men came onto the stage and helped the richest poet to stand up. The large room swayed as he was helped to the side. This is a device known as transferred epithet. The room didn't sway; it was the richest poet who swayed. But because he was swaying, the large room seemed to be under his influence, and it swayed as well. Knowing about such matters can help you see how powerful poets are, even when they are very drunk.

This was a perfect moment to make myself known to New York City by reading my poem about Fay Trigger. The fat girl was still standing on her chair. She said this to me as I moved past her seat to the aisle:

"That man has more charisma than a roomful of presidents, even when he has the DTs." Then she said this: "Hey, toad, you forgot your bag."

This was true. But I could no longer reach my seat, for at

that moment the poetry audience began to flow toward the exit doors. I was pushed backward by several old women. One of them asked me: "Did you ever?"

The fat girl in the raincoat was calling to me from somewhere in the crowd. She had lifted up my suitcase filled with socks and poems and was shouting at people to let her get through.

The old woman who had spoken to me before spoke again when the fat girl arrived, shoving people out of her way with my suitcase. She said: "I never."

The fat girl dropped my suitcase on the marble floor of the lobby and said this to me:

"What you got in there, dead chickens?"

"Poems," I told her.

"Yeah, right," is what she replied. She took out a cigarette and lit it. Something about this reminded me of Fay Trigger.

"I am a poet. And now that I find the richest poet in America is very ill with alcoholism, it appears I will be needed."

She coughed smoke and said, "Riiiight." We watched the people pouring out of the auditorium.

"I shall take the richest poet in America job, since now it seems to be open."

She dropped her cigarette and ground it into the marble floor and stared at my eyes in a manner that Fay Trigger often used just before she was about to say, "And a pig was ice skating to the Blue Danube, too." This device is new to me.

The fat girl in the raincoat said this:

"Everybody in this damn building is a poet. This town is lousy with poets. There're more poets here than sand at

Coney Island, and you think you're going to score big. What gives you that idea?"

What she said to me was news. Bad news. I said to her:

"You are using hyperboles, please tell me, or some device new to me."

"Wow," is what she said. "Wow, what a royal goof."

I felt a great whale wallow inside my chest. This is a pun. Something happened to my eyes.

"Everyone here is a poet?" I asked her.

"Everydamnbody in the United States of America is either a poet or trying to be."

This seemed to include Fay Trigger. I wondered if Fay Trigger had been, perhaps, loving me so she could learn the secrets of poetry from me. The whale sprouted a funnel of water.

"And you without speaking English better than a beaner with his shirt still wet . . . What a goof!"

It rose up out of the deep blue water of my soul and thundered its tail against the surface of my ocean.

I spit on the back of my hand and rubbed the words there, making them a blue smear.

The fat girl in the raincoat spun around quickly and pulled a man out of the crowd. He looked very shocked. He wore a tuxedo.

"Can you give a reading of your poems tonight?"

"What time?" he asked her. She pushed him back into the crowd.

"You see what I mean? You could yank anyone out and they'd say the same."

Across the marble floor I carried my suitcase of socks and worthless poems. The fat girl followed me to the door of revolutions and stood in my way and said this:

"Even the muggers, friend, even the rapists, even the damn hookers are staying up late writing poems. You don't have a prayer. Listen, I know. I teach seven-year-olds to write the stuff. And mongoloids. I mean mongoloids, for Christsakes.

"I mean, it's an insult to me and to all of us, especially to him tonight, to say you can come walking out of nowhere and become a hotshot. No way, José. That man has worked his ass off to be up there tonight. He's the real thing. The real king. There aren't twelve people in the United States of America that understand every single nuance of what he says. He's the deepest, friend. The very deepest."

I replied to her in words she could not pronounce.

And she regarded me with far-off eyes like I was on the deck of a departing ship. I felt myself pull free from the great country of America where she stood surrounded by the swarming poets. I felt myself cut out into the marble sea, into the fog of my own impoverished language.

Into a language where the important things are the simple things to say. You say them plainly and in a way that causes no one to be unsure and no one to need an explanation. You can turn to an old woman with whiskers on her chin who is selecting peppers from the vegetable bin, and you can say to her, "These tomatoes and peppers smell tasty." And she will understand you. And you, you will be rich.

AN
AMERICAN
BEAUTY

◾️ ◾️ ◾️

*H*is barber had told him that if he got to be thirty-three without losing it all, he was safe.

"How can you know? My father, brother, grandfather have nothing left. Even my mother's thinning out."

"Listen. I've been cutting heads for thirty-nine years. You pick up a few ideas in that time. And I never seen it fail. You make it to thirty-three, and what you got is what you'll go out with."

Duriel's birthday was the Fourth of July, and he had planned to take Judy to Sandy Key for a holiday cookout. It was a forty-five-minute ride in his whaler across protected water. Then five minutes across the edge of the Atlantic. A real desert island. In five years he'd never even found a beer can there.

The wind had lain down nicely as they'd cut across the dark green swatch of ocean and seen Duriel's island inflate into view.

"Oh, Duriel."

"Just wait!" he shouted up to her. He was manning the outboard, woozy from inhaling her coconut suntan oil and from watching her oily breasts wobble from the light chop.

Judy dove into the water as Duriel beached the boat. He unpacked the gear, and Judy called to him, her suit floating into shore. He was about to skin out of his own suit when he felt a burning tingle on his dome. When he touched his scalp, he bellowed, and July nearly drowned splashing to shore. She was choking badly but managed to ask what was wrong.

"I'm bald! I'm bald!"

"Oh, quit fooling around."

"I am! I am, look, I'm bald."

Judy was rolling her suit back into place over the white cutouts.

"Judy, Judy. Oh, Jesus, oh, Jesus. I'm bald."

"Settle down, Duriel. Please."

"I might have made it one more day. Thirty-three today, and today's the day it all falls out! Good God Almighty."

She looked at him as though he had spoken in tongues.

"Hon, you've been bald since I knew you. Years. You've been bald for years."

"I've got a sunburn, too."

Duriel bowed at the waist to show her.

"Holy shit!"

"What! What is it?"

Judy kept mumbling under her voice while she located her purse between a palmetto scrub and the Coleman cooler. She withdrew her compact mirror and trotted back to him.

"See?"

She shone the mirror on his scalp, but he couldn't see.

"It's cute," she said. "Kind of."

"What the hell is it?"

"I don't know. Maybe it's some kind of cancer. Something."

"Jesus Detroit Pistons!"

An hour later Duriel stared at the pouting cicatrix in the boathouse men's room. It glowed like radium. It was like three sets of lips that had kissed him around an axis.

Monday Duriel didn't show up behind the counter at the automotive parts store. He sat in three waiting rooms.

The earliest his own physician could see him was August 31. He found a Pakistani doctor who would wedge him in in three weeks. So at six-thirty he drove out to the Sears Town shopping center where his barber worked. His head was smoldering, but he was afraid to touch the gruesome welts. His barber smiled when he entered.

"I was thirty-three yesterday," said Duriel, falling into the chair.

His barber tied the paisley apron against his throat.

"I see."

"I missed it by one day."

The barber adjusted the chair, pumping Duriel higher.

"That's the first one of those I've seen in a long while."

"You know what it is?"

"Not exactly."

"But you've seen something like it?"

"No, no, this is quite uncommon these days."

"But you just said you saw something like this once."

"Usually you get jonquils these days, or I've seen a couple of crocuses lately. But this is . . . I'm not sure." The barber snipped some stray hairs near the pout.

"Jonquils!"

"No, this is no jonquil. No, sir, this is a rare old lady. I'd say it's some kind of rose."

Duriel tilted his head, looking up at where the Little Dipper would be without the barbershop.

"This is fatal, isn't it?"

"Sure, sure. Now I recognize it. It used to be a big item. It's a Madame Ferdinand Jamin. One of those old American Beauties. But its color is a little weak. Still, it should be a healthy one."

Duriel was growing wistful. His eyes were muddy; the barber's mirrors were misting over. A fine haze burned the edges of the brass cash register.

"It's fragrant already." The barber pulled his nose away as Duriel straightened up. "If I was a young man like you, I'd find me a nice girl who liked American Beauties and have some fun with her. You could get a lot of ladies with a rose like that."

Duriel was unaccountably thinking of a shipment of spark plugs he'd unpacked before the holiday. He was screwing one of them into the socket in his head now, feeling it nestle neatly into place. Alive, powerful.

"It might come as a surprise to you, young man. But when I was your age, I had a black orchid that had them oozing under my door at every hour of the night. I made Engelbert Whatshishump sound like a bag of peat moss. I was as bewildered as you are right now when it first peeked through. And fortunately I went, like you, to my barber.

"He gave it to me straight, told me how to keep it in bloom, about light and moisture. You know, that's why I become a barber. You find most all us scalpers got our start that way. Bewildered and then pissed as hell when we learned the truth. All that wasted time worrying about that black orchid, hiding out, thinking I needed cobalt treatment. But my barber gave it to me straight.

"It's a flower, is what he told me. Not one to mess around. It's a flower, and a flower don't last. It's the beauty of it that it don't last, and that's the pain of it, too. There'll be some who won't understand, who'll want you to wear a wig, a hat, anything so you look normal. But no, sir, my barber gave me the word, and I'm giving it to you. You got to learn how to tip your head, son."

Duriel looked at the barber's bowed head, at the faded afterglow, a delicate shaded patch like the wings of circling birds at dusk.

"Enjoy it," said his barber. "Learn how to tip your head. I think you're going to have a prizewinner there. If you treat it right."

Duriel reached up. He edged near the wound. His fingers touched a calyx and a quiver fired down the back of his brain. A zipper opened down his spine. Spark plugs crackled. The Little Dipper emptied into him.

When he could, he said, "I just didn't know."

"Just ask," said his barber. "That's why we're here."

THE
MIRACLES

I

I'm calling this "The Miracles" because my name is Candy Miracle, and him over there sucking on a warm beer can is my husband, Elwood Miracle. You might think when you pick this up that it's about some kind of Bible miracles or such. But no, it's all pretty down-to-earth, pretty normal really, even though the parts about everybody getting mesmerized at the football games might seem awful farfetched.

I'm getting ahead of things now.

Here's another beginning.

If when I tell you I work at the Cadiz Beauty College out on the New Smyrna Road, you say to yourself, well, that must be what her story's about, her tacky little life in a backwater town in Kentucky, you just made a mistake. Most people around here don't aspire to nothing greater in life than being a beauty operator, and having the heads of people in their hands all day every day, but I do. My goal is to write this story. And write it right. I only got this one good story to tell, and I figure that being the perfectionist I am, it might take me the rest of my pitiful life to tell it.

That's right. My life is pitiful, and this is going to be a depressing story. I know a lot of people can't stand reading that sort of story, 'cause they had a mother or a baby up and die on them, and one more tragedy doesn't seem inviting. So this is for those others that are building up to their big tragedies, haven't had them yet, but want to maybe get a little taste now to get prepared.

Now a lot of people around here would find it funnier than a pig up a peach tree that Candy Miracle was trying to write up her life story. Coach Thornton would laugh till his stomach came out of his mouth and blew up like a balloon. But it isn't funny a bit, and the reason is sitting over there. Elwood, staring off into his poor dead mirrors, without having one idea in his damn head. And it isn't funny 'cause I'm over here at our little rickety secretary pretending to write a letter to my grandmother in Florida when what I'm really doing is trying to keep all this from swirling down the drain.

You probably didn't get what I meant when I said Elwood was in front of his mirrors. I got to go way back now, back to when Elwood Miracle first came home from college, knowing everything there is in books but not having sense enough to butter toast. And he moves into the old Miracle place where he was born and raised, but that was abandoned and condemned. His people had disappeared just after he left for college. Everyone in Cadiz knew he was inside there and all, but no one bothered him 'cause it'd been his daddy's house.

And he slept upstairs. His room was decorated with a Japanese globe that you could see when you drove in the drive-in movie that was built next to his old place. And if you drove slowly and were lucky, you might see him pacing past the window. He'd been hiding out up there for a couple of weeks, creating rumors and giving all of us shivers as we'd stand primping in the bathroom, talking about him. He was about the only thing mysterious in all of Cadiz. Been there two weeks and already he was magic to me, and then all at once I was looking him in the face.

Coach Thornton was introducing him to me, but I didn't catch but a word now and then, 'cause I was looking up at Elwood. Red, curly hair, and eyes as blue as the swimming-pool water at the Country Club in Hopkinsville, and big ears that looked like little hands that he'd cupped up there to hear someone arguing in the next room. He was looking off somewhere, at the lockers or into the home ec lab, which was a good thing because I needed a minute or two to get used to him. Then Coach snapped his fingers in front of my face once or twice, and I came back.

"This here is Elwood Miracle, Candy, as I been telling you. He's the class of '62. Elwood's a college boy now, and he's come home looking for work. He says he's good with words and whatnot, so I'm renting his educated services to give you cheerleaders an opportunity to improve your cheers this year. I'm thinking we need to dress up our appearance this year, since with Thud and all there's a good chance we'll be playing for the state championship, and I don't want us embarrassed by doing the same old two-bits four-bits stuff. So, if Elwood here wants you girls to do push-ups or whatever, you just do them. You hearing me there?''

"Yes, sir.''

"Another thing, Candy.''

"Yes, sir.'' I was still scrutinizing this Elwood Miracle.

"What time does your mama want you indoors of a Saturday night?''

"She doesn't say any time exactly.''

"I'm going to tell you something then, just between you and me. Thud has got to be in bed asleep by nine o'clock every single night. So if you two plan on going down to Teen Town or wherever, I'd be much appreciated if you'd get him moving on home sometime before then.''

"Yes, sir.''

"We're playing Franklin-Simpson in that first game in two weeks, and Thud, between you and me, needs his sleep before he butts heads with those ham hocks.''

So Coach finally left, and there we were. Elwood staring off at everything and nothing, like he was trying to recall something that happened a long time back and me standing there holding this awful painful smile. Finally the late bell rang and the hall was empty except for us, so I said see you later and scooted on to health class.

I saw Thud Thornton, my steady boyfriend, after lunch that day. He wanted to go out and sit in his car and feel my breasts, but I was still shaky from meeting Mr. Mystery, and I told him no.

"I'll get them sex bumps,'' he said, spreading his huge shoulders out.

He always got sex bumps if he couldn't feel me every day.

"I can't, Thud. Not today.''

He was mad and hurt, but all at once, for the first time ever, I didn't care a bit. I didn't care if the best fullback in western Kentucky dropped me. He turned around and headed on out to the parking lot to sit and listen to his radio, I guess, and I felt a sigh come out of me that seemed to make me twenty pounds lighter.

That afternoon the other girls and I were out on the football field, painting some old tires white to use for yard markers, when Elwood came across the cinder track and stood right in the middle of us.

"My name is Elwood Miracle, and I am to be your teacher."

"I'm Candy," I said. "You remember me. From this morning?"

"And I'm Sandra."

"Me too."

"So am I."

"I'm Sandra, too."

"Yeah, we got four Sandras and a Candy," I said, and the other girls looked Elwood over from tip to top. Just then there was a real loud growl from on the field and a smack of leather on leather, and a helmet came rolling up almost to Elwood's feet.

He picked it up by the face guard and waited till Thud came loping over to get it. He'd knocked it off some fellow's head, and Coach made him come over to return it.

"Who's the creep?" he asked me, taking the helmet from Elwood.

"My name is Elwood Miracle. Who are you?"

"Thud Thornton, all-state fullback."

"That's nice," said Elwood. "I'm pleased to see that you blacks have penetrated so far into the elite sectors of this

provincial town. It's unfortunate that you must permit yourself to be exploited in such a savage manner, just to accom-
plish your social goal."

"Whud he say about black?" Thud asked me, while looking puffed-up mean at Elwood.

I told him Elwood was just jibber-jabbering college talk
and for him to scoot back to practice. It was a good thing I
was there 'cause Elwood was about to get his skull pow-
dered. What do they teach in colleges? Maybe to talk, and
sling your fancy dan words around like custard pies, but
good Lord, a loon would know better than to call Coach
Thornton's boy a Negro.

I mean, he is dark, has fat lips, kinky hair, and a flat nose
and all. But there isn't anybody would call him a Negro to
his face. He's Puerto Rican, Coach Thornton says. Coach
adopts a good big dark boy every few years, gets them from
somewhere, Puerto Rico, I guess, brings them to Cadiz, and
gives them a car and a good high school education. And I
never heard anybody around here objecting to it. Anyway,
if Thud was a Negro, they wouldn't let him go to Cadiz
High. He'd have to go to Booker T. like the rest of them.
And my mother sure wouldn't let me go out with him.

I told Elwood this, and he only laughed. I swear the air
changed seasons when he laughed.

Then he asked us to do our best cheer. We did "Red
Hot," the one where I do the splits three times. We were a
little awkward, but my last split was real good. Elwood just
smiled like he'd seen something he shouldn't have. He kept
watching me. I was the only blonde on the squad, though I
do bleach it now and again to keep it looking right, and I
thought it must have been that blond hair that kept him
watching me, 'cause the Sandras all had better bodies. After

we finished, he just stayed there, sitting on a stack of old tires, smiling like he'd just woke up from a good dream.

That weekend Thud and I were at my church's picnic down at Jeff Davis Monument when I saw Elwood again. Thud and I were laying behind a thick hedge, and he was trying his best to convince me that he might die of sex bumps unless I did something quick. I saw Elwood through a little split in the hedge. He was looking up at the monument like people does when they first see it. I stood up quick and picked some loose grass off my sweater and told Thud I had to go talk to *my* coach.

"No, Candy, I swear I'm getting them bumps on the inside of my brain. It's eating at me."

"Poor Thud," I said as I pushed on through the bushes.

I knew something was wrong between me and Thud. Usually his beefy hands left this lingering trail of excitement, as if they were coated with analgesic balm. But since Elwood had appeared, his hands were just boards. It made me sad. And it made me wonder if maybe boys sweated some kind of acidy stuff when you loved them, and when you didn't, you could feel the way they usually were, rough and scratchy.

I walked up to Elwood where he was still standing, wobbling a little from looking up at that huge monument. I stood there looking up at the bottom of his chin, until finally he noticed me.

"It's a wonder," he said. "It's a sheer wonder how a man who was president of the Confederacy could generate such a graceful and elegant sculpture."

"It's a monument, is all it is," I said. "Not really a sculpture."

148

Unfolding a piece of paper, Elwood gave me a sleepy smile again. Then he told me he'd written our first new cheer.

This is an important part. I don't know if I can get it just right, but here goes.

The air was getting cool, 'cause it was late afternoon, and the leaves had just begun to smell that different way. It was a Saturday, and I felt chosen. I felt like the sky would roll open if I just called out for it to.

Then he recited that first cheer in his burning voice. I listened carefully, and I felt my sinuses suddenly spring open. Except my sinuses were in my brain, and instead of just sucking in a lot of fresh air, I sucked in everything.

I don't remember when he left. I just stood there without moving, listening to the late-afternoon birds and the little children playing games, and the air felt like it was inside my skin, and the smell of new-cut grass and of burgoo and fried chicken was almost all I was right at that moment.

I try to tell this in the Beauty College and the girls act like they're under the hair dryer and don't even nod that they heard. It makes you wonder if people are able to say anything to another person outside of "Pass the sugar" and have him understand.

So the moon rose, and it was gigantic like the sun, and everybody got quiet and I guess some of them were looking at it. And then there were hymns from up at the pavilion. I'm sure there were gnats and mosquitoes, but I wasn't feeling anything bad. Or I was switching everything around to a good thing. I could have been standing in a hill of fire ants.

When the singing stopped, it got quiet except for cars leaving the parking lot. And then my mama calling my name, and Thud with her calling, "Candy, Candy,

Caaaandy." I hadn't moved an inch when they found me. I was still where Elwood left me. They made a big fuss and I went with them, but right there at Jeff Davis Monument I realized there was a heap more to being alive than eating burgoo and singing hymns.

I was scared and swallowed a lot, 'cause I thought that maybe everybody else already knew about this feeling and that it was what everybody sang about, wrote poems about: I thought it was love.

How wrong I was.

You get far enough from the earth and they say the air gets sparse. That's how it was with me. I was up there, way up there, looking back down at myself, thinking I was taking a full, deep breath, thinking I was in love at last, when fact was, I was running out of oxygen. And it was making my head swim. If I'd just been able to stay inside my own body, see what was in front of me, smell what was up, take a good, hard look at what was about to run me down, I might've had a prayer. The problem was, I expected love to be spectacular, something so wild and different that it would clobber me. I had no idea how quiet a thing it is.

II

It started to rain on the drive home, and the thunder sounded worse than I'd ever heard it. One kaboom just rumbled into the next one. It sounds crazy, but I felt like I was making it storm like that. Like I was thrashing the clouds into one another, making those puffs of lightning explode inside a thick muffle of clouds, and sending streaks of unholy electricity sizzling toward the earth.

There was Thud pouting in the back seat, hulking, crossing and uncrossing his leg. Shuffling and snuffling. There was Mama, squinting at the Fairview Road, bent forward toward the wipers, frowning. I thought, Who is she? I thought, Who is that boy back there? He doesn't even belong to our church. Who is he that I let touch my breasts? Why him? The thunder kept grumbling like one jet plane passing over after another in some Second World War movie. The wipers were slapping, and I felt like the car was being pumped full of air.

There was too much air in the air. Who were those people and where were they driving me to? What had I done that made them mad at me? And the airplanes kept coming over, and over, and the car couldn't hold much more air. I was awful sad about that cheer Elwood recited. Awful sad now. Seemed like somebody had just walked up to me and said, "Candy, you don't have one thing in the entire world you believe in. Candy, you clap and cheer for football games, you sweat over books for homework, you do what your mama orders you to and what Thud whines and whines you into doing, but you don't believe in any of it. You don't have nothing solid in the whole world to stand on."

There was just too much air in the car. So I swung open the door and looked down at the wet pavement flashing past. And I jumped. It didn't hurt.

Fairview Road was wet and it was hard and it was moving very fast underneath me. It rolled me over and over, but it didn't hurt at all. And the car drove on without me; my door flailed like a loose shutter. I didn't scream, not out there in the rain and dark and lonely wet. I didn't scream because it felt so good to be alone and to not have Thud

asking, "Did I do somethun? Don't you like me no more?"
And no Mama saying, "Candy, you best start thinking seriously about after high school, who or what you're going to
be doing. You aren't a little girl forever, you know." I
didn't scream until later.

That Friday night we used some of our last year's cheers.
And I had bandages all over me. Even one on my lip. But I
still did the triple-split "Red Hot." The pep club cheered
loud, which made me happy, but when the game was over,
we'd lost by one point and nobody felt much like going to
Teen Town. Thud's daddy made the team stay after and run
laps, so I went off hobbling home.

I hadn't gone a block from the stadium when out from
behind a tree steps Elwood Miracle.

"We lost," I said quick before I said all the other things
I'd been thinking about.

"Only temporarily."

"How's that?"

"After tonight the Cadiz Flamingos will never lose another game."

"I hope not."

"I can assure you of it."

"Franklin-Simpson isn't even as good as Madisonville
will be."

"The Miami Dolphins won't be able to beat them after
I've taught you those cheers."

I didn't say anything 'cause I could see how sure of it he
was.

"And football is only the beginning."

He was so lathered up about this that I thought I better
stay close to him to keep him from walking right into some

headlights. I fell into step beside him as he went on about how nobody had to die in wars anymore and how there were hundreds of ways he could use this discovery for man's benefit.

Poor Elwood. Poor, poor man.

The drive-in movie next to his house was showing a scary double feature. The projector must have been set off kilter because there was a sliver of the movie that was missing the screen and was playing against the side of Elwood's house.

Before I'd decided what I was going to do or not do, we wre climbing some rotted stairs inside that house. The old Miracle place had lost most of its roof in a fire ten years back and was just waiting for a strong wind to flatten it for good.

"I'm sure those new cheers will make a difference," I said, trying to break the tightening quiet.

He didn't say a thing until we'd climbed all the stairs and were standing inside his room. Then, if he'd said a word, I wouldn't have heard it, 'cause I was staring away at the lights and the mirrors.

The room was filled with mirrors, broken scraps twining and untwining on strings hung from the ceiling, big panes of mirror glass leaning at odd angles against the walls, more pieces tacked on the floor, the walls, on the footlocker, on the closet doors. And that slice of the drive-in movie was coming in through the window and was batting and shuttling around the room in all those mirrors. It was like being inside an electric sign. You couldn't tell what part of the movie it was, 'cause it was just color and it kept changing.

Elwood led me over to his bed.

I couldn't see him clearly because of all the splintered light. But when he reached out and slid his hand under the bottom of my letter sweater and glided it along the band of my skirt, I knew there was nothing I wouldn't do to keep that hand on my skin.

He ran his fingertips across my ribs, and then a finger painted a simmering path next to my bra strap. He paused at the hollow between my breasts, left a fingerprint there in the dampness, and then went on to my other ribs. I knew I was breathing too loud, sounding unladylike.

He explored the tingling skin between my shoulder blades, and without a bit of trouble, he unlocked my bra. But he wasn't any Thud, going straight away for my nipples. Elwood let the loose bra stay there while his hands went on their luxurious trip. When one of his fingers touched the thin skin just inside my hipbone point, I swayed back away from him and moaned for him to stop. I was dizzy from the lights. I had gone off somewhere else. My eyes had turned nearly backwards.

Then he began peeling away the bandages.

After he peeled one off, he would kiss the place where it had been. I had a jillion of them all over me, and he found every one. The last one he peeled off was the one on my lip.

We folded up inside his sheets. His hands molded me, slid up and down me, smoothing out the skin. I don't remember touching him at all. I just lay there watching that light stitching across the ceiling, feeling my shoes come off, my white socks, my black wool skirt, the scratchy sweater, the loosened bra, and then the cold nylon of my panties.

"Elwood? Elwood, are you OK?" I asked when I thought he'd stopped touching me. Then I saw he was still there, naked himself now, pressing his long, slender body against mine. I felt larger than myself, and I didn't feel him touching me.

I hate words. I hate their feeble-hearted little selves.

A bird woke me. It had flown through a broken window

and was smashing into the mirrors, fluttering straight at one, bouncing off it, sitting still, dazed, then bursting up again to get out of the room. I got out of bed to help him, but the mirrors had so many birds in them, I couldn't tell which was the real one. I sat back on the bed and watched for the bird awhile, until finally it sailed right into one of the mirrors across the room and disappeared right into it. Seeing something like that before breakfast made me nauseous.

I was cold and sore, and there was a car honking outside, too. And Elwood was gone, and to make matters worse, there was a blue light flashing outside the window.

It turned out it was Mama and Thud and Holland Darnell of the local police. Mama was arguing at Elwood, who just stood smiling at her in his blue jeans, his white shirt, and barefoot on that October morning, not saying a thing back to her. I wish he'd bit off the finger she was waving in his face.

Thud was looking sad as a mule and staring off at one of the windows on the other end of the house where he must've thought I was staying. And Holland was watching Mama shake her finger, and he was playing with the whistle on the leather cord around his neck. Holland used to be an extra-point kicker for the Cadiz Flamingos a few years back. He was so forgetful about things, though, that Coach had to Magic Marker *Left* on his left foot and *Right* on the other one. He'd always get mixed up about the steps and kick with the wrong foot and the ball wound up sliding off into the bleachers or hitting one of our men in the back. It didn't matter much back then, though, because that was in the days before Coach started bringing in the dark boys to score touchdowns.

Finally Mama and Thud drove off in her car, and Elwood

and Holland had a chat. I put on one of Elwood's long-sleeve shirts and sat down on the footlocker next to his bed. All the mirrors looked crazy and naked there in the Saturday daylight. I wondered what in the world I was doing. I'd never so much as stayed out after eleven o'clock before and here I was staying the weekend and maybe forever with this magic man. I took a great gulp of air when I heard him coming back up the stairs.

Monday morning Elwood drove me to school. I was still wearing my letter sweater, which was OK since it showed school spirit in the face of a losing game. Well, when I got out of the car in the parking lot out behind the band room, there was Thud, and there was the principal, Mr. Weavers, with him.

And there was half the football team, too, and three of the Sandras, each of them whispering and grinning at me at once. There was about half the rest of the school out there, too. It looked like some kind of awful pep rally, where Elwood and me might turn out to be the effigies.

Thud looked blank, but I saw that finger-size vein he had in his neck which was always a real bad sign. He had this size twenty-three neck, which I remember 'cause I had to order his Christmas shirts in the middle of summer. So anyway, I'm standing on one side of the old Ford; Elwood has gotten out the other side and is standing there with a smile that looked dead serious. And Thud walks away from beside Mr. Weavers and comes right up to Elwood. The principal and everyone except Thud's daddy let Thud do pretty much whatever he wanted 'cause he was an all-stater when he was just a sophomore.

I said, "Thud, you hurt that man and I won't ever look at you again. I swear I won't."

That seemed to hold him up. You could see him and Elwood were mingling breaths, and it still wasn't over by a long way.

Mr. Weavers came over to me, looking confused.

"Tell the fellow to get on back home or wherever," he growled at me.

But Thud had already given up on trying to make Elwood blink and was walking over to me. He looked at me hard, and the crowd started to budge up closer. Then he stared at my breasts so obvious I thought I might slap him.

"You let him touch those?" he asked. "Did you?"

Poor Thud.

I guess I must have looked pretty guilty 'cause that snaky vein rose up again, purple and explosive.

All of a sudden Thud spun around and took a giant backswing and punched Mr. Weavers in the belly so hard he staggered back three yards or so into the three Sandras.

Thud stalked off through the middle of the crowd. It was mighty embarrassing to see Mr. Weavers gasping and spitting up. The crowd drifted off, but there were a lot of them that took one more look at Elwood as they left. He couldn't have asked for a better way of getting known to everybody right off if he'd planned it.

At cheerleading practice that afternoon Elwood taught us the first cheer. Before he began, he took out lots of little mirrors that he said we were going to be using instead of pompoms. And then out of his beat-up satchel he pulled our cheers, which he'd printed in his own handwriting.

He handed them around. We were on the first-row bleachers across from the practice field.

"Look them over," he said.

"I can't read it," said Sandra right off, pouty.

"It looks like smeared roach pellets," said Sandra.

Another Sandra said, "I bet you every vocal cord in Nashville this is supposed to be a joke."

"It's a joke all right," he said. "But don't fool yourself into thinking you could ever fathom it. All I want is for you to learn how to do it."

"I quit," said pouty Sandra.

Elwood ignored her and began to explain the cheers real carefully. It seemed crazy to me, but the other girls began to settle down and go on with him. He said how the words were some of them Latin and some from other languages, and that not to worry that no one would understand them outright. They would feel them, know them down deep. It sounded like school, college even, harder than any subject they had around Cadiz. But I stuck in there for Elwood's sake.

He showed us how to use the mirrors like he wanted, and had us sing with him two or three notes, flashing those mirrors out at the football field. It sounded shivery, like a Negro funeral late at night in the woods, and it reminded me of the feeling I'd had out at Jeff Davis Monument. The more we sang it, the more it felt like I'd snipped my fingernails off too low, all over my body. Like my whole brain was fingernail-quick.

When we got back to Elwood's that night, I was feeling low again. I thought maybe it was the way you felt when you were in love. While Elwood sat down on the bed and folded up his legs under him, humming to himself and watching the mirror lights, I watched out the window the double drive-in screen that I could see through the trees. Things were just getting going over there, with some dancing popcorn bags and talking mustard jars.

I said, "Why'd you latch on to me, Elwood? Any girl in

Cadiz would be crazy about you. What's special about me anyway?"

He raised his head up from his humming and gave me a lazy smile.

"I like the way you never ask me questions about my art or questions about why I selected you."

"It's making me sad not knowing what you see in me."

I sat down on the bed beside him.

"Candy," he said, and he took my face in his spidery fingers. "Candy . . ." You could tell he was winding up to let fly with a fastball. "I like you because you're the least special girl I've ever met. You're the common denominator. You're the Muncie of women. If anyone can help me find my reference point again, you can. I see in you a shopping mall of clichés. You are middle C, Candy, neither out far nor in deep. And for a long time I've been out on the teetering edge of the cosmos, and now I want to stand at the fulcrum again, where I can begin to integrate what I know into normal terms. You, Candy, are normal terms."

Oh, he talked on and on, and I bet I'm mixing up his words right and left. But it makes me queasy and dizzy to remember all he said. A good half of my brain stopped dead on that "Muncie of women" thing. I was trying to remember if Muncie was a capital or a famous producer or some important car, or maybe the home of a president. I was giving myself a lot of credit. But he went on holding my face, talking to me like I was a lump of limestone he was trying to convince was alive.

Come Thursday and time for our first auditorium pep rally, I knew those cheers inside out, and I also knew something was weird about them. For one thing, Coach Thornton had made us start practicing cheerleading down at the

Baptist softball field 'cause the humming and flashing of the mirrors had made the players start just standing around listening and moping and drifting off. Elwood bought three dozen earplugs out of his own money and offered them to Coach, but Coach just told Elwood he reckoned the team could stand listening to those cheers if everybody else could. He talked to Elwood like he'd made a big mistake hiring him, kook that he was turning out to be.

But it turned out Elwood was right, and lucky for Coach he found out at the pep rally. Coach Thornton stood up on the stage underneath the tilted-up basketball goal and introduced the team. Everyone got cheered real hard except for Thud, and they just went nuts stomping their feet and rattling chairs and whistling when he walked out. He still walked slow and edgy like he was carrying a bomb inside his shirt.

Then we came out in our new purple and yellow outfits with Elwood wearing his old Cadiz High band jacket. We were going to teach everybody this year's cheers. Most everyone knew by then who Elwood was, and there was a lot of whispering and talking just before he spoke. He started off talking about how cheerleading was an art. And a bunch of seniors thought he was being funny and laughed. So then he talked about cavemen and how they changed their luck by using songs and about some people who lived in China and who traveled back and forth between different planets by singing a certain way.

People started scraping their chairs, talking some, a couple of spitballs sailed, and finally Elwood gave up and decided to let us start. And I thought, God, the pep's gone out of them now, how'll we ever stir them up?

The Sandras got their mirrors out and I got mine and we

sat down cross-legged on the floor and started moving the mirrors around like Elwood showed us and began humming cheer number one. Everybody out there seemed amazed and got very quiet. Nobody caught on right off. But after a minute or two you could hear some of them begin to do it back.

Well, about seven-thirty that night the fire department came bursting in through the doors in the back of the auditorium, and there was Holland from the police with them. And everyone in school was still sitting there. Some of them had begun to use mirrors from their makeup kits or just shiny gum wrappers. It was fireworks. The firemen rousted everybody, and most of them got up real reluctant like they'd been asleep, which they sort of had been, and they marched like drunk people to their lockers. Mr. Wallace, a history teacher, refused to budge. A couple of firemen had to tote him out to his car, and he was still humming those cheers.

Coach came up to Elwood and me out in the parking lot.

"I'll be taking you up on those earplugs," he said. He was looking confused and sleepy. Elwood promised to bring them on the bus the next day. We were playing an away game over at Madisonville.

When we got back to Elwood's house, Mama was sitting on his front doorstep.

"Candy," she said, "you are a whore and a trashy, trashy woman, and you're going to die of hideous diseases if you don't come home this minute."

"I'm not some little girl," I told her. "Elwood and I are getting married soon as football season is over. He already asked me and everything."

She started crying for real when Elwood began to explain

how I was everything a man could want in a woman. Then she called Elwood a name I didn't know she knew, and grabbed hold of me and hugged me hard and left.

That's not exactly all we said. I said some things about how Elwood was an important person, and about how the world was going to be Utopia after Elwood's message started getting around, and how a winning football team was the best way for him to get his start. I said a bunch of things like that, but it seems stupid now to have said it, so I'm just leaving it all out.

III

It was a couple of hours over to Madisonville, and the bus was quiet as a coffin. Coach wanted everybody to be thinking about Madisonville, our worst rival.

Every year there were bloody fights in the stands. Last year Harold Wiggins got his ear bit off by a fourteen-year-old girl. I had gone back to the pep bus with him, and he carried the ear that the girl had given him back after spitting it into the dirt. In the bus we tried taping it back on but finally gave up and went back to the game and left the ear in the team doctor's ashtray on the bus. You couldn't trust any Madisonville doctor. He might've sewed that ear back on crooked or in the wrong place.

So now Harold only has one ear and a ragged hole that looks like a Florida seashell. So I was thinking about poor Harold and all the players were quiet and probably thinking of times in the past when Madisonville had beaten us and about the dirty fighting and the bad referees and the way they always pelted the bus when it came under the railroad trestle outside town.

Elwood was snoring, his head bumping against the window. I suddenly felt like an old married woman. It was like in just two weeks of living with Elwood I already knew where he liked to touch me best, how he was going to kiss me and for how long. And I'd already felt him on top of me driving away, and it hadn't felt any better than that day Thud's hand felt like a board. I said to myself, Candy, you got it all. This man is way beyond anything you could ever come across again, and what are you doing? You're acting like you want something more. But I did. Lord, I wanted something more.

And it was those cheers made me want it. I looked over at him, a book bouncing around in his lap, and I swear if I didn't half hate him for ever having made me feel so good once.

Then we were in Madisonville's big drive-in restaurant for our steak dinner before the game. I sat with Elwood and the Sandras over near the front window, and everyone in the restaurant was talking about us. One tall fellow with a turtleneck sweater came walking over like he was ready to start something. He got to our table and stood behind Elwood's chair.

"You boys must be the first team."

The men at the table he came from all laughed real mean.

"We're the cheerleaders," I told him.

"Roughest-looking bunch of cheerleader I ever did see."

Coach Thornton was standing behind the bully by then. His big stomach brushing the bully's bottom.

"Excuse me, sir," Coach said.

The bully ignored him and said, "You people got your plumbing indoors over there yet?"

Coach put his arm around the man's shoulder like they were old friends. But the bully's eyes went slack, and he and

Coach turned around very slow. They were on their way out the door to the parking lot when Elwood popped up and yelled for Coach to hold it.

"Come on, girls," he said to us.

We followed Coach and the bully out to the parking lot, but the Sandras weren't sure of the wisdom of it. At that point I would've followed Elwood into a penful of mother pigs.

We stopped beside Coach, who was still holding on to the bully. Everybody in the restaurant was pressed up to the window. A few of the fellow's friends were hanging back by the door to see how rough we really were.

Elwood said the name of a cheer, and we all looked at him puzzled.

"Do it," he said. "There's a better way than punching this guy in the face like Coach was about to do."

"Face, hell," Coach Thornton muttered.

We got our mirrors out of our purses, and Elwood gave us the signal and we started chanting.

That fellow in the turtleneck let his eyes drift up toward the sky, kind of smiling, and Coach, though he'd heard that cheer a dozen times by now, let go of him, and his face went soft and dreamy.

By the time Elwood stopped us, there was a crowd of moaning Madisonville hoods swaying around us in a ring. You could've picked the straight razors right out of their pockets, emptied their flasks on the street in front of them, and they wouldn't have minded at all. That Elwood!

I don't care how bad it got because of him; he made it better than it ever was before.

We won that game 83–0, which was the score in the second quarter when their team finally stopped moving around and the referees had all sat down grinning and chuckling and looking off at the night above the floodlights.

The bus ride home was awful. It was quiet like after a losing game, only worse. It was like nobody had really won anything, except maybe Elwood. And then, too, I think everybody was just as sad as I was that the chanting cheers had stopped. It was a deep letdown.

Elwood sat next to the window again, and he pointed the little ceiling light at a book he'd brought along. It was about dead people in Tibet, and it looked to be in a different language to me. I suddenly thought that maybe Elwood was stealing those beautiful cheers from another football team over in Tibet, and that upset me plenty. So I asked him straight out where he got those cheers from, and he said he found them deep inside him, but I wouldn't go for that and asked him how they got inside him, which made him smile and look at me for a long time until I wanted to cry and kiss him and yank away all at once, and he said they're in everybody, all of us, which surprised me 'cause I'd never felt them inside me till Elwood showed up.

"Why the mirrors?" I asked. "And how come the drive-in movie?"

"So many questions."

"It's your job and a wife should know what her man does on the job." That was feeble and I knew it, but I couldn't come right out and say I was worried he was stealing those cheers.

Now what he said then makes me dizzy just to try to remember it. He tried his best to explain about movies and mirrors, but he was speaking Brooklynese far as I could tell. It was something about how when you go to see a movie that lasts two hours, you'll wind up sitting in the absolute

dark for about forty-five minutes. Especially at the Princess
Theater, I thought, 'cause the projector's always broke.
And those dark frames, he said, were the moments inside of
moments, like the second between when you breathe in and
breathe out. And he said his cheers were just the dark left-
out sounds that no one ever heard, but when they finally
did, when they are forced to hear them, they feel this bliss-
ful awareness, this clear, deep river of peace.

I remember the "clear, deep river of peace" part real
well, 'cause when he said it, I thought of Ox River, where
Thud and I had gone lots of times the summer before. And
then I felt worse than before. And what did Elwood do
then? You'd think after spilling out all these secrets, he
would've taken my hand in his and kissed me, or done
something to say he was feeling close and safe with me. But
no, he flopped open that book again and disappeared into it,
flying away to Tibet, I suppose, leaving me to try to un-
tangle all those tenpenny words alone.

IV

It got around western Kentucky pretty quick that Coach
Thornton's Flamingos had something up their sleeves. But
not a one of those teams we put into the clear, deep river
and then thrashed let on to any other team in the state what
was coming their way. I guess they wanted their chance to
laugh at such lopsided scores. Or maybe they just didn't
even remember what it was made them feel so fine and
woozy.

Anyway, Elwood stayed busy in the mirror bedroom
coming up with new cheers from the river of peace. And I

stayed busy thinking how I could have a bigger share of this man I had opened myself up to.

Those cheers affected everybody. The sports people at the *Cadiz New Era* took to being weird. Instead of writing the scores of the games or what happened play by play, they'd put in a song they wrote or draw a picture of some pasture with a creek running through it and cows relaxing under shade trees.

Principal Weavers let us have pep rallies every day, starting after lunch. I didn't know anyone in all of Cadiz who'd miss a pep rally. Even a bunch of the hoods came and sat in the back rows, elbowing each other and smoking cigarettes until the hum got going and the mirrors were splitting the light like the sun had just exploded. Then you'd find them at about six o'clock that evening as happy as caboose drivers, using their knives and brass knuckles as reflectors.

Elwood, of course, was a hero, and even Mama came over to the abandoned house to call upstairs that I should come down and get some cake and roast she'd made for us. When I was down there, she said she reckoned that I had been right about Elwood and that we had her blessing. I hugged her, but I didn't tell her how hot and cold I was for him and all the rest, the cheers and all.

There we were, riding the tide of the highest wave that ever washed into Cadiz, and I was Elwood's chosen woman. I could have walked into any store in town and walked out with everything nice and no one would have thought twice. They acted like I deserved anything I laid my hands on.

But something wasn't right. Like the night at Jeff Davis Monument when I was first washed over by those cheers and happier than I'd ever been before, there I went jumping out of the car like I was trying to kill myself. Like I didn't have any right to all that peacefulness that was welling up in me.

And it was a lot of people around town looking mopey, too. Like they couldn't wait for the pep rally next afternoon, 'cause the world looked awful mean and scary between pep rallies. You could walk up to an old friend on the street and try to say hidey, and they'd flinch like you'd screamed in their ear. The later into football season we got, the touchier everybody was becoming. We were next to undefeated, except for that first game before the cheers, and every boy on the first team was getting college scholarship offers, but there didn't seem to be anybody but Elwood really enjoying it.

The night after our last regular-season game, which we won 159–0 over Clarksville, Elwood told me he was going away for a couple of days. He showed me his airplane ticket to Washington, D.C., after I laughed at him. I thought it was a joke. He couldn't leave just before our first regional game with Madisonville. Those boys would be sure to be protected against the cheers by now. He couldn't leave till he found something that would bust through their earplugs.

He just said, "Football is nonsense. I chose football only because of its ritual connection with warfare. This is going to win us more that a state championship. In case you have forgotten, dear girl, there's a larger arena than the Flamingo Bowl." With that he left.

It was three months before he made it back.

By then most everybody had woke up. We got smeared over at Madisonville. Thud had both of his legs broke. There wasn't one of our boys who hadn't got so out of shape during the fall that when those mean Madisonville boys wearing big earmuffs started tackling and blocking, there weren't enough stretchers in the county to carry them all. We hummed our cheers loud as we could, but no one heard a thing except a few blackbirds and bluejays that came swirling down to sleep in the end zones.

Before he got back, some man over in Princeton, who was a little bothered we'd mauled his son's team earlier in the season, bought the land where Elwood's house was and knocked it flat. I didn't even get a chance to rescue the mirrors or his books. But by then I wasn't sure he was even alive anymore.

I moved in the duplex half next to Mama and started working out at the Beauty College and hoped the women who sat down in front of me would someday stop saying nasty things about Elwood deserting Cadiz in our time of greatest need. Everybody in town scowling around for months like they had one exploding hangover.

Then, one night, I'm getting out of Mama's car smelling of hydrogen peroxide as usual, and there's Elwood. He had a beard and his hair was all snarled and his band jacket was missing a sleeve. He tried to stand up when I ran over to him, but he was so far gone drunk that he fell flat forward and lay in the jonquil bed.

"Oh, Elwood! What in the world's happened to you?" I helped him stand up and faced him toward my duplex door.

"The Pentagon," he said. "The bastards, comfffrr . . ." and then he just fell forward into the doorknob. "The mo-therfudg . . . And had a waaaaaay." He was crying, and Lord, if all at once I didn't feel free of him and loving him more than ever both at once.

I got him inside and laid him on the couch, and he kept

on sputtering about the generals and the government and about how the human condition was never going to change. How everybody's imagination was locked in stone. A lot of other things I can't repeat or it'd make this pornographic.

Mama left me alone with him, and I smoothed his forehead, a lot like he'd done to me that night when he took all my bandages off. I kissed him and tasted all the bus stations and bars and cigars for three months.

The next week, when he was up and moving around and had begun to eat a little again, I brought home an armload of mirrors from the Quick Drug. We spent all night breaking them up and arranging them around the room in as near a replica of his old room as we could both remember. He was foaming up with happiness.

"What'll we do about the drive-in movie?" I asked.

He looked at me sad and dropped onto the couch. "I forgot," is all he could say. "I forgot."

When I came home next afternoon, he'd pulled all the mirrors down and his hands were all cut up and he was sitting at the kitchen table drinking about his thirtieth beer and listening to Chubby Dink give the farm report.

I can't go on.

Nothing much has happened since that afternoon. Oh, I married him. I can't tell you why. But I felt like I owed it to him somehow. And there was the Saturday morning when half of Cadiz showed up outside the house, most of them with rotten vegetables and eggs. There's the night he tried to buy a bus ticket out of here, but Holland caught him and lugged him on back home. All it would've taken was for one person to recognize him in this part of the state and he'd get pelted with more than vegetables.

And there was the night I refused to go out and get another six-pack of beer and he stood up out of the kitchen chair and came over to me, mean and crazy-looking, and said, "Candy, you must have forgotten the great joy I gave you and every other person in this banal town."

"No, I haven't. Not a minute ticks off that I don't wish I could some way leap back to the way I felt before you ever stole away my mind. I thought you must have been Christ himself coming home, back then. I did, though you smile now. We all thought it. And here it is you were selling snake ointment, is all. Sugar water."

"It wasn't," he said. "It was real."

"Thud Thornton would be busting heads today at East Kentucky, instead of sweeping out the pool hall. You stole his guts. And you stole mine."

"Get me another beer, or I'll hum a cheer."

I keep him in beer all day and all night now. I think I'm doing everybody some kind of favor. The faster they all forget, the better. But then, just when you think you've forgotten about how it was to dip down into that clear river, somebody says something about mirrors or Band-Aids or Jeff Davis Monument and it all comes swelling back.

And here I been thinking all through this terrible time, cramped up at the secretary, that I'd built me a stepladder out of all these words and I could climb back to that room and see those lights shuttle and blaze and hear Elwood dragging up some more of his ecstatic moaning. And I could rest on that bed again and take Elwood into me and feel larger than the room, larger all of a sudden than that house, all of Cadiz, bigger than the county.

But it doesn't work. Don't let anybody ever tell you it does. Writing this thing has got me hand cramp, is all. All

JAMES WILSON HALL was born in western Kentucky in 1947. He attended Eckerd College in Florida, where he studied with Peter Meinke. He earned his M.A. from Johns Hopkins University and his Ph.D. from the University of Utah.

He has published four books of poetry, three with Carnegie-Mellon University Press, *The Lady from the Dark Green Hills, The Mating Reflex,* and *False Statements.* His poems have appeared in many magazines, such as *Antioch Review, Poetry, Georgia Review, North America Review,* and *American Scholar.*

He has also published short stories in such magazines as *Iowa Review, Missouri Review,* and *Carolina Quarterly, Kenyon Review.*

He was a Fulbright professor in Bilbao, Spain, in 1979–80. He is a professor of literature at Florida International University in Miami.